MESHA MESH
PRESENTS

That
DOPE LOVE
WON'T SHUT
Me Out

D'ASHANTA

That Dope Love Won't Shut Me Out
D'Ashanta

Mesha Mesh Presents Is accepting submissions!
Do you have a finished manuscript? If so, we're looking for authors in the following genres: Urban Fiction, Street Lit, and AA Romance. Please send a three chapter submission, synopsis, and contact information to alluremepresents@gmail.com. We're also offering bonuses for experienced authors.

Dedications

First and foremost, I want to thank my Lord and Savior. Without you, I would be no one.

Mesha and Deshon, y'all mean the world to me. Y'all have helped me glow up and I'm glad I chose this family to be a part of.

Magnificent seven: Jap, Blac, Keedie, My Guy Ty, Big E, Bodie, and Kamster words can't explain. Aside from being a part of the great eight, Big E is the master of all of punchlines and metaphors, thank you my baby.

Jade, Christina, Pammy, Krissy, TN Jones, and my fans thank you for pushing me to the limits to stay in the game. Mom, thanks for grooming me to be who I am and to never be a quitter. We are definitely going places... see y'all at the top. MUAH. R-Dub, love you son.

Allure Me squad... y'all know what it is. Dominique, u know what it's hittin' fa babes!

To the Riley family, know that you all are in my heart and prayers. Darren and Pooky, thank you for being characters on this journey... Long live Pooky Riley.

In Memory Of:

Dontrell "Doc" Jackson

May 21, 1992 – December 7, 2015

Gone But Never Forgotten

Big Sissy Loves You Forever!!!

Table of Contents

Synopsis

What is love? That was the million-dollar question. If someone presented ten stacks of one-hundred-dollar bills before me to answer that riddle, I'd lose it all. I couldn't say what it was, but I could most definitely describe in detail, what it wasn't.

My name is Dominique Johnson, known to family and friends as Nique. I'm a trust fund kid who aspires to prove to everyone that because I was born into money, it didn't define me nor alter the fact that I'm humble. As a teen, I had love all mapped out. I knew what I would and wouldn't accept nor tolerate from a man. My idea of a partner was cut and dry, until the day I met a guy named Spencer. Everything I knew, had jumped out of the window. The rules of love had changed.

His New York accent along with his swag had me smitten. I was so head over hills for this man that I took his infidelity and covered the bruises just to keep him. My unwavering love and loyalty to him had me second-guessing my own sanity at times. After giving him five years of my life, he betrayed me in the worst way. It wasn't until he gave me an STD, that I knew love wasn't shit.

My motto from that day forth was simple, Jazmine Sullivan said it best, "Why do we love love when love seems to hate us?

Chapter One
To Know Me Is To Love Me
Dominique "Unique" Johnson

J ust as I exited the stage from my performance, a peculiar voice yelled my stage name. "Unique, Unique, I know you hear me calling your name. Are you just gone walk past the nigga that been dropping hundreds on your ass all night long?" he called out to me.

As I turned around, I recognized him to be one of the regulars and I really didn't want to be bothered. Stripping was my job, I did this for the meat and potatoes, and so that I didn't have to depend on a man or my parents. True enough, I fulfilled many men's fantasies, whether it was a regular lap dance, or a personal dance in the privacy of what we coined The Purple Room. Nonetheless, I had a nothing ass nigga at home. I couldn't stand thirsty ass dudes, he stood there demanding me to come to him. He was tripping if he thought he owned me, I didn't ask him to throw all his hard-earned money on the stage.

I was an only child and my parents didn't spare any expense when it came to what I needed or wanted. I had top-of-the-line everything, even nannies. The few guys I had dated broke up with me because they considered me to be shallow or materialistic. However, their accusations were far beyond the truth, they simply couldn't handle me. I was merely a woman who wanted and deserved the best. If the person of interest wasn't comfortable enough in his finances, and couldn't give me what I wanted, I could become pouty and petty.

Sometimes, I may have belittled their manhood. Oh well, they should have stepped their financial game up. There was too much currency out here for a man not to be able to take care of a woman like she deserved. I would never settle, that was until I met Spencer. I gave him what separated the teenaged girl from womanhood, my virginity. When I crossed that line, it changed my thought process as far as what a man should provide for his woman. It had gotten to a point where I didn't even demand his loyalty. I guess you could say I had been dickmatized.

I couldn't help that my parents were well-established in their careers before they decided to start a family. My mother, Cassandra Denise Mills, was twenty-six when I was born. She was the head of the accounting firm the she worked for. Not much later, she became partner because of the accounts that she landed and the hard work she'd put in.

Sadly, it was her dream, even if it meant leaving me to be practically raised by my nanny. Fortunately, the time she did find to spend at home, she spent every moment with me and my daddy. Therefore, our relationship flourished as one would with a domestic mother that stayed home with her kids daily.

My father, Ronald Dominic Johnson, was a military man. After he had served four years in the Marines, then went to college, where he met my mother. He was five years my mother's senior, which left my grandparents feeling as though he only wanted to brainwash and control her. That was far from the truth, today everyone knows who wore the pants in our home. Daddy was thirty-one when I was born, and he'd been settled in his own publishing company for six years by then. He was a big name in both the fiction and non-fiction world. He even published his own magazine *Dominic's Way,* which had been a hit for the past nine years.

I stood five feet, seven inches and weighed one hundred-sixty pounds. I had a small waist, thick thighs, and my tig ole bitties were a C-cup. I kept my hair dyed jet-black and it was naturally wavy being that my grandmother was an Indian. A real Indian from India, not Native American, which people seem to get confused. I never understood how Natives were mistaken for Indians, they didn't even look alike. That's neither here nor there.

As the regular customer approached me, I bit the inside of my cheek. It had been a habit of mine since I was a girl.

"What's up Byron? What can I do for you?" I inquired with an attitude hidden behind my inviting smile.

"You know what it is. A nigga wanna get you in the Purple Room," he smiled devilishly. Something about his smile and demeanor didn't sit well with me. Because of my sixth sense, I tried to think of an excuse not to oblige his request.

"I just got off stage, I would like to clean up first," I smiled. "I know you don't want my sweaty ass all on your Rokker Violator's huh?" I suggested, referring to his five-hundred-dollar jeans. I believed they were the same jeans he wore last week, broke ass nigga.

"I don't give a fuck about these jeans. I've been coming here twice a week every week. A nigga been dropping a lot of loot on you Unique, I'm trying to see what that Purple Room action be like. I heard it goes down back there and I got plenty of money to get what I want. That's you."

My eye started to twitch, as it had always done, to somehow warn me of something about to go down. "Look, I don't know what you heard Byron, but I'm not like the rest of these dancers. Whatever sleezy shit you heard about them, doesn't apply to me. I don't make niggas holla for a dollar and I don't do shit strange for a lil' change." With disgust written all over my face, I turned to walk away.

Thinking I made a clean get away, I didn't realize Byron was on my heels until I made it to the dressing room door. He grabbed my arm aggressively and I saw the devil in his eyes. Snatching me into his grip, he grabbed me by my neck and slammed me into the wall with his right hand.

"Bitch, you trying to play me, aren't you? I'm not a stupid ass nigga like the rest of these fuck boys. I have seen you go into the Purple Room plenty of nights without changing. I spent over ten stacks on you since I been coming to this raunchy ass club. Either we fuckin', or I'm fuckin'."

I laughed so hard at that statement. Not because I wasn't afraid, but the way my mind was set up, I immediately thought of the meme that was floating around social media in lieu of the Bill Cosby case. I guess my laughing pissed him off because he tightened his grip.

Licking my neck with his sticky tongue, I felt his hot breath that reeked of alcohol while he rubbed his rugged hand up my thigh. That area was very sensitive, and I hated for anyone to touch me there. Both my legs were covered in tattoos, no one ever noticed the long scar that ran along my outer right thigh. If you weren't a friend or family, you didn't know a scar was there.

I had an accident in my younger years that left me screwed up mentally. Part of me still believed that my ex-best friend had a death wish and attempted to kill us all. God had other plans. When I turned twenty-one, my best friend Sharae, who we called Latrice because she hated her first name, our other best friend Victoria, and I drove up to Lafayette, LA to party with the ballers. Every week we heard about a club called 337 on the radio, now that I was old enough to get in, we went there and got sloshed.

On the way home, she decided to 'catch the drift' of an eighteen-wheeler and cut another one off. Cutting too soon, it was a pit maneuver and our car got mangled on the Atchafalaya Basin bridge. That was the absolute scariest night of our lives. Had our car toppled over the side of the bridge, with all the blood that was leaking from us, the gators would have feasted and none of our remains would've been found.

Hearing the door to the dressing room open and my arch rival, Halo's voice, I snapped back to the present. With the reality of being choked and attempting to be raped staring me in the face, I kneed Byron in the nuts with all my might. That form of defense caused him to loosen his grip and I made a break for the nearest security guard, so they could throw him out on his ass.

One thing C-Note didn't allow, was for anyone to disrespect his dancers. Disrespecting us was disrespecting him. His mother was a go-go dancer, he respected us for what we did because he knew the life and the business. With that being said, if the dancers wanted to go the extra mile in the Purple room, that was their choice. There were a few of us with a little pride and dignity. We didn't do the extra crackhead shit like suck and fuck for a buck.

After they had gotten rid of the problem, I showered and donned a black *PINK* sweat suit with *PINK* written in diamonds on the leg and across the chest. On my feet were a pair of custom Air Force One's that I copped from Da Sneaker Peddler, and a few pieces of jewelry.

I hung around awhile, afraid that Byron would be outside waiting for me. Sure, I could've had security walk me to my car, but I would rather Big Wyatt follow me home. Once we made it, we could have a drink to make sure that my personal environment was safe. Being that Spencer was supposedly out on a delivery, I would be home alone for the next few days. That nigga swore he was the plug. All I could see was him plugging the next bitch's pussy with his stinking-ass dick, because I sure wasn't fucking him.

Wyatt, the bouncer at Purple Haze, the club I worked at, was sexy as fuck. He was an inked up white boy and was very appealing to the eye. All the dancers referred to him as White Chocolate. He was real smooth. If I wanted him, he'd be mine by now. The two things that stood between us were the fuck nigga Spencer, that I had dedicated the last several years of my life to, and the fact that he was white. I liked guys that looked like my father, not racist by far, just in tune with melanite brothers.

"Hey, you ready to dip?" Wyatt walked up questioning me like he was a boss.

"Boy, you running up on me like you my man," I laughed causing Wyatt to smirk. His dimples did something to me.

"Look girl, I don't have time to play with you. Am I following you home or not? You always sending mixed signals and shit. With your beautiful ass," he replied.

"Yes please. That crazy ass Byron might be waiting in the shadows for me, since I got him kicked out."

"Aight, let's go, ma."

$$$$

"Are you gonna come inside for a few minutes? I wanna be sure I'm straight, ya know." Honestly feeling the need for protection, I played it safe.

"I ain't trying to have no qualms with Spence. I don't do beef and especially not over women. It's not my cup of tea," Wyatt stated. It stung a little bit. It almost made me feel less worthy for him to say he wouldn't beef over me.

"Look, I ain't tryna start no shit. The only person that owes him loyalty is me. It's not like we're going in here to have sex, I just want to have a drink and make sure everything checks out before you leave. Supposedly, he's out of town anyway."

"Cool, just know that I'm not with all that drama, Dominique. I work, make beats in my studio, and chill with my homeboys. I don't have kids, I ain't married, and I keep out of trouble. Don't misquote me, I'm not scary by any means. I just don't like that dude to rear his ugly head. Ya mean?" he asked, allowing his New York accent to come out thick.

"How do you know my government?" was all I could ask at the time.

"I know all the dancers' government names. I like being in the know, is all."

"Oh, so you're nosey huh?" I laughed and walked to the bar with him in tow. "What will you have to drink?"

"What can you make?"

"Anything. Ever heard of Tipsy Bartender?"

"The Facebook page?" he queried.

"Yep. I follow the Facebook, I'm subscribed to the YouTube channel, and I pin every pin on Pinterest. I am a beast behind this bar. I should be a barmaid, but the money is in the dancing." Smiling because I felt liberated to make my own money and be my own woman, I grabbed two glasses. "Now, what will you have?"

"A grown man's drink," he smiled.

"Strong, sour, or sweet?" I probed.

Most grown men wanted strong, but he was white. Maybe his grown man drink was different from a black man's grown man drink. Call me ignorant, because I surely didn't know if there was a difference or not.

"What kind of grown man wants a sour or fruity ass drink, Dominique? Make sense. Don't be crazy girl, shit," he educated me, and I felt some type of way. I guess a man was a man.

"Well, excauuuuse me then, mister. Dark or clear? I don't think I have ever seen you drink."

"You probably haven't, because I don't drink on the job," he half-smirked.

"You have a mouth on you. I don't know if I can deal with your snide comebacks," I informed him. Still not sure if he drank what black guys drank, I made him a glass of Evan Williams on the rocks.

"Deal with me? You serious too, huh? Girl you crazy, fa sho. You don't have to deal with me remember, we're co-workers," he sipped his drink and shook his head. "This my shit girl, how'd you know?"

Chapter Two
"I'm The Man In These Streets"
"Spencer "Spence" Hines

T ake this dick and stop running, la bitch. You was talking mad shit when I was spending all my bread on drinks in the mufuckin' club, yo,"

I pummeled my uncircumcised pole into the nameless woman that was on all fours in my hotel room.

Grabbing the back of her neck, I slammed her head down into the mattress and used my other hand to lift her ass up. She was gonna take this dick like a big girl. Her fine ass was built like a woman on the outside, but the pussy was tight as a fuckin' virgin.

Sobering up at the sight before me, I spoke. "Aye, you a damn virgin, yo?" I asked. Looking down at my condom, I took notice of the streaks of blood that covered my Magnum XL.

"I was, but I guess I'm not anymore," the familiar voice eluded through sniffles.

Recognizing who she was for the first time, I noticed it was Lestlee, Latrice's baby sister. Latrice was my girl's ex-best friend. It was still unclear as to what they had fallen out behind, but I didn't give a fuck. With them being at each other's throats, I had the best of both worlds. Latrice was a freak in the sheets, nothing was off limits. Not one hole went unstuffed. I think I put my dick in her ear once. Nique had to be taught to please me and it still wasn't gratifying enough. Thus the reason I am here, fucking a new bitch.

I sat in the chair near the window and stared at lil' baby before me. I was mad as fuck because I didn't want the attachment that came with virgins. True, I was in Miami, but this chick was from the city where I laid my head. My hometown was Queens, New York. I moved to Baton Rouge, LA to attend Southern University being that I wanted to be an alumni of an HBCU. Plus, I wanted to be far away from New York after me and the only nigga that ever really had my back, fell out over me fucking his lil' sister's thot ass.

With her eyelids and cheeks covered in makeup, blonde hair, and the skimpy ass clothes she sported, I hadn't paid attention to anything beyond her physical. Namely, her face. The only features I took in were her phat ass, her titties, and the fat pussy print that sat nicely in her Pablo jeans.

"What the hell you doing in Miami, hanging out in a club, that you ain't old enough to be in?" I was confused.

"I am old enough to be in the club. I'm not old enough to drink, but since you were buying, I never got carded. I am a student at The U." It was then that I remembered Latrice flying with her sister down to the University of Miami, for freshman orientation. "You act like you didn't know who I was," she said, breaking me from my memory.

"Well hell, I didn't. I don't look bitches in their face if they fine as fuck. It wasn't until I heard your voice, that I knew who you were," I admitted.

"What you doing in Miami fucking random bitches you meet in the club? My sister and Nique ain't enough pussy for you?" she smirked.

"If you knew about me fucking your sister too, why you busting it open for me?" I quizzed.

"Tricey's the reason I don't have Nique in my life. I've always respected and loved her more than my sister. Because of her and her bullshit, Nique is gone now," Lestlee said. "I might as well see what got both of their heads in the clouds, right?" she added. "Hell, I want my head to be in the clouds too. So we gonna finish what you started or what?" She got on her knees and took my meat into her mouth.

My shit immediately hardened up. I was a fucked-up ass nigga, my mind was telling me not to do it to her ass, but my dick was saying 'Hell yeah, two sisters and an ex-best friend'. *Nigga you winning*, I thought. So of course I took the winning route.

"Damn girl, where you learned how to suck dick? I wanna drop hundred-dollar bills on your back while you slurp a nigga up." Her pussy was a virgin, but her throat, jaws, and tongue were a pro. I guess she sucked niggas off and denied the pussy. "Get your ass up there so I can eat that pussy up before I beat that pussy up." She sucked a few more times and obliged my request.

Her pretty little untouched pussy was about to get stretched every way but back into shape. The thing about virgins, was that their pussy fit like a glove to my dick. I loved that shit as much as I hated it.

That was the reason Dominique's duck-ass was so whipped. I could do anything to her and all she'd do was cry and cuss me out. She had a couple boyfriends before me, but I doubted they honed the experienced dick-game as I did. Shit, I doubted they had even fucked. She said she was a virgin and as tight as her pussy was, I believed her. I was five years her senior and I controlled her every thought and every move. She was as weak as they came.

"Look lil' baby, I don't want no attachments. I already got two crazy ass bitches in my ear. I'm warning you lil' girl, don't blow my phone up, stop by Nique's, or call Latrice looking for me. Understood?" I spoke while rubbing the head of my monster up and down her shaven, soaked, throbbing pussy lips.

"Fine. I'll do whatever you want. Stop teasing me with that dick and fuck me like a grown man. It seems like you're the one that needs rules. After tonight, this never happened between us."

That shit pissed me off. I shoved my dick in her so hard I felt her pussy rip as she screamed out in agony.

"Don't play with me, lil' girl," I said and kissed the side of her face where the stream of tears was. "Breathe, baby. With you holding your breath and tensing up, it's gonna make it harder on you." She took my advice and relaxed her muscles. It was on from there. I found myself making love to her like she was wifey. The fact that I knew I was the first one in that pussy, made me comfortable enough to finesse her juice box well into sunrise. I was worn. After washing up, I fell asleep like a newborn baby.

Afternoon had crept up on me. After handling my hygiene, I checked out my chocolate frame in the full-length mirror. I was one sexy tattooed muthafucka with biceps and triceps for weeks. Bitches flocked to me like moths to flames.

Walking over to the table where my jewelry was laid out, I noticed a piece of paper. I couldn't believe she left a 'note on the dresser' for me. "I had a great time. Thank you for everything. Be easy, Lee-Lee," I smirked and shook my head.

Perceptually, I was the bitch and she was the nigga. "Well ain't this a bitch," I spoke aloud in the empty hotel room.

****

Finally touched down in Goon's Town, or Baton Rouge, I couldn't wait to see my bitches. I know they gone hook me up with pussy and money. I was that nigga. True enough, I made plenty of money doing my delivery thang for Shiggy, but even too much money was not enough when you a greedy Queens nigga from the bricks like myself. I was known for chasing the bag.

Walking to my black Mercedes Benz GLS 4matic that sat on twenty-two-inch Borghini B19 Chrome rims, I thought about life and how I had prospered over the years. True enough, I had women carrying me, but in all honesty, I had my own crib that I had bought for when I needed to clear my head and be alone. My girl thought I lived with her and drove a Toyota Tundra. Gullible ass bitch.

Most of the time Domi thought I was out fucking someone else, I was laid up in my dual-king-sized bed watching my wall-mounted seventy-inch LED television. I felt accomplished like a muthafucka when I was at 1089 South Burgess. I owned over fifteen-hundred square feet of home and over four-thousand square feet of land. All I did was pay taxes on that shit every five years.

Settling inside of my car, I felt uneasy. I got out and did a walk around in an attempt to make sure there were no visible damages to my whip. Not seeing anything out of the ordinary, I decided to hop in, start Lucille up, and head to Domi's. It was Sunday evening, so she should have been home.

As I pushed the door open, she stood, vacuuming the floor in boy shorts and a tank top. She looked sexy as fuck. My dick rose to the occasion immediately. Bopping her head to whatever music she was jamming to from her earbuds, she hadn't noticed me enter her apartment.

I walked up to her and kissed her neck. She didn't seem surprised by that action. Hell, I didn't even think she was happy to see me.

"What's up babe?" I queried as she removed the ear buds.

"Ain't nothing, just doing my Sunday ritual. I've meditated, meal-prepped for the week, and now I'm cleaning. What's good with you? How was your trip?" she asked with a resting bitch face.

"You act like you ain't happy to see a nigga," I responded not answering any of her questions. "You fucked a nigga while I was gone or some shit? Huh?" I walked up to her, grabbing her pussy through her barely-there shorts. "Bitch, you giving my goods away?" I growled while forcing my finger inside of her to check for tightness.

"What the hell is wrong with you, Spence? Every time you cheat you come home tripping and accusing me of the foul shit you doing out there. I don't give a damn anymore, I'm over your shit, my nigga," she replied.

"Bitch, make me smack you down up in here. You know I don't give a fuck about you sporting a black-eye. It's invisible under that clown-ass makeup you cake on your face," I threatened.

"Look, can you do whatever you're gonna do because I need to finish cleaning my crib? I'm meeting my parents for lunch today, per usual..." She glared at me. She was taunting me. If she wanted me to fuck her up, I had no problems sending her to mommy and daddy with a black eye.

"Who the fuck is you playing with, girl. I'll choke you to sleep. Keep it up with your smart-ass mouth. That's the reason we don't get along now. Duck-ass hoe," I had her by her throat. She didn't flinch or wince.

Usually, she'd beg me to stop, cry, whimper, show some type of inferiority. This time, I didn't feel dominant. I felt like I had lost my touch on instilling fear into Dominique. I detected she had detached herself from the reality of what was happening. She stared through me with soulless eyes.

"Can I finish what I'm doing so I can take a shower? I'm over this shit with you. I have given you all of me and all I got from you in return was gonorrhea." With that admission, I was beyond pissed.

"Bitch," I yelled and slapped her so hard, the bun that sat atop her head became a side ponytail. "If I got gonorrhea, I'mma kill you. I don't have no symptoms, so that means you gave it to me not the other way around."

"You really did that right now? *You* slapped *me* for giving *me* an STD? You can't be serious!" she yelled. "I've only slept with one person my whole life and that's you, nigga!" she admitted. I gotta admit she held her ground, not one tear fell nor did her hardened demeanor.

I knew she hadn't stepped out on me, her pussy was always tight and fitted to my magic-stick. It was my only defense for allowing myself to slip up with a slut and catch some shit. I wouldn't slap the one who burnt me because she might stab my ass.

"Go get ready for your date with your parents. If I find out you on some fuck shit, you dead," I threatened and walked into the guest bedroom.

The only bitch other than Domi that I had slept with without a condom what that whorish ass Latrice. Deciding to shoot her a text, I sat on the chaise and pulled out my phone.

Me: Aye, you might wanna get checked.
Message sent 13:01

MGP: What the fuck I might wanna get checked for?
Message received 13:03

I had to think of something to say. I would never speak to her the way I spoke to Domi. Tricey was a queen, there was no way she would enable me to get away with half the shit Domi did.

MGP: ???
Message received 13:07

MGP: The fuck Spencer, cat got your tongue? Don't drop no shit like that and get quiet.
Message received 13:15

I knew Tricey was gonna flip out. She was gonna swear I'd been sleeping around. In truth, I had been. However, I wore a condom with the other hoes I was fucking at the time.

Chapter Three
"You Ain't Never Seen A Hurricane Like The One I'mma Cause"
Sharae Latrice Joseph

"If I hit it one time, I'ma pipe her
If I hit it two times, then I like her
If I fuck three times, I'ma wife her."

I basically mumbled the song because all I really liked was the chorus any way. I lived my life since I was twelve, fucking niggas, getting money. I wasn't new to this shit, I was true to this shit. I didn't give a fuck if they were straight, bi, lesbian, black, nonblack, tall, short, married, nothing. If their money was long, a bitch was sure to suck and fuck for a buck.

Before you judge me it was all I knew. My mother was a drug-addicted whore who began selling me to grown-ass men when I was eleven. I figured if she could sell my pussy for her needs, I could sell my own pussy for me and my sister Lestlee's needs.

Lestlee was born when I was four. I took on the role of her mother by the time I was six. No woman in their right mind would have a six-year-old making bottles, changing diapers, and caring for themselves and a two-year-old so they can run around riding dick and getting her ass beat on the regular. Sadly, that's the type of mother I had. Word on the street was, my sister was also my cousin. If that was true, that was some nasty, trifling-ass shit and she needed her ass beat for it.

With what I'd learned over the years, I knew how to get enough money to pay the balance of the rent since we lived in public housing, pay the electric bill, buy food, and buy our clothes and school supplies. Shiiit, mama wasn't doing it, so somebody had to.

After all of the years that I'd been protecting Lestlee from the streets, more so, our mother, she had finally graduated high school. Being who I am, I made sure she didn't go to college here so that all my hard work wasn't in vain. Our mother had a way of getting in a muthafucka's head. Lestlee was down in Florida, attending the University of Miami, also known as *The U*. All of my days of coming home to a snotty-nosed, shit-filled diaper, whining child were worth seeing her do the Shiggy dance across the stage. I had never felt more accomplished.

"Fuck with me and get some money (ayy), Fuck with G and get some money..." The lyrics crooned from the Pink Pill that I had talked Spence into buying me. That nigga

was a duck, he thought I loved him. Naw nigga, if you fucked with your girl's ex-best friend on some fuck shit, I could never love you. To be honest, I don't even trust his fuck-ass. If I knew one thing about relationships, I knew that how you got them, was how you would lose them, and I didn't come to lose.

Yep, I was fucking my ex-best friend's man. Fuck that hoe, she deserved it. People thought we fell out because I fucked Spencer. Truth is, I didn't get that dick from him until after she stopped talking to me. If you ask her what we fell out over, she'd say it was because I stole fifteen hundred dollars from her. The reason for the fallout was she was a privileged bitch and I hated her ever since we were kids. She didn't lose her virginity until she chose to. Her parents loved her, whereas I didn't know who my father was, and my mother only loved what I could provide.

That friendship was privy to ending anyway. We were on two totally different levels.

I snorted another line of coke off the vanity I sat at while caking on make-up to get on stage. Yep, I was a fuckin stripper in one of the hottest clubs in the city, Purple Haze. When I started this job, I was a simple-ass bitch. All I knew how to do was fuck a man and get some money. Attaching myself to one of the OG's of the club, I started drinking and snorting cocaine to make the reality of my life easier to deal with. At least that's what I told myself.

I sang out loud my favorite part of the song, *"Tell your man pipe up, Nigga pipe up, Hunnit bands from the safe, In your face, what'd you say?"* I threw my hands in the air and grinded my hips like I was working hard to get a nigga to get a few stacks outta his safe. These niggas knew, when they stepped to me they had better come correct. I wasn't no cheap bitch, I didn't fuck for a Michael Kors bag, a bitch fucked to pay her mortgage and I don't own a house yet.

"Alizé, you up next. You loose-pussy back-stabbing hoe," Halo, one of the baddest dancers on the roster, spat at me. She knew I wasn't a fighter, so she'd take shots at me every chance she got. The bitch talked mad shit about me one night when she saw me and Spencer together at the Waffle House. After Dominique started working at the club on weekends only, she'd see Spence there picking her up. From time-to-time, she'd also hear us talking about him. She knew he was Nique's man. I don't know why it bothered her as much as it did, she didn't like Nique anyway.

"Thanks," I said. She stood behind me, looking at me through my mirror with a disgusted scowl on her face. "Why do you hate me, and you don't even like Unique?" I queried.

"Bitch, I hate you because you dirty. And as far as not liking Unique, don't assume shit. I don't fuck with her because I don't know her. There's a difference. Finish up your poison and get your community pussy ass on stage before C-Note comes back here trippin'. When he trips, I trip," she mushed the back of my head and strutted in the direction of her locker.

Cardi B had just finished her verse, I was bucked and ready. These hoes ain't 'bout getting this money like me. I was about to go out there and dominate the stage, make my round of lap dances, and likely end up in the Purple Room giving some random the best head he'd ever had in his life. I called it the pocket drainer. Cha-ching, it was time to cash out... "Fuck a man and get some money," I said to my reflection.

"Money, dance, Turn this shit into a nightclub, Fuck him then I get some money, Fuck him then I get some money." ASAP Rocky had me pumped up more than the coke and the Hennessy that I'd consumed in the last hour.

After snorting another line of coke, I headed towards the stage. I was feeling like Ms. America and ready to take on the mixed crowd. One thing about C-Note, he didn't care about your gender or race, as long as you were there to spend money. I popped my pussy in the women's face for the most part. They would dominate the stage with tips, therefore, I would give them a show.

I made it to the stage and *Real Sisters* by Future started to play, giving me an adrenaline rush. I always used it as my introduction because thirsty niggas fed on bitches that liked bitches.

Climbing the pole, I rode it like a cowgirl to a horse. I dropped down in a split just as Future screamed, *"Oh, that's your best friend, I'm tryna fuck her with you. First met the bitch, they said they real sisters, I don't give a fuck if they was real sisters. Fuck around with me, you tryna dodge bullets."*

The stud looking chick walked up and smacked my ass with a stack of bills, then dropped them on me. For that, I gave her a real show. I laid flat on my back, busted my pussy open, and made my thighs clap. In turn, that made my ass cheeks clap together, causing the crowd to go wild. Money was flying at me left and right.

At the end of my set, I headed to the Purple Room with the same bitch that was throwing her money at me. It was gonna be the first time I had been in there with a woman. Mind you, I had been with several women and it's safe to say I'd rather slang that strap-on to a bitch than ride a dick, any day.

"What's good witchu?" she asked.

"I'm good ma, what you looking to do?" I replied.

"Shit, I'm just tryna see what's poppin'. What you tryna do?" she asked.

"Shiiit boo, I'm tryna get this money."

After all was said and done, all she wanted to do was talk about her relationship problems. I wound up being her listening ear and she wound up breaking a whole lot of bread. Before I left, I kissed her and told her everything would work out, and if it didn't then she need to work on something else. One thing my mother always said was: *In the end, it'll all be ok and if it isn't ok, it's not the end.* Life wasn't ok for me yet. I guess I wasn't near the end.

Walking out of the Purple Room, Jessica's girlfriend was on the other side of the door. Before she said anything, I knew some drama was about to pop off. Because we go into the Room that has an emergency alarm button near the seats, there wasn't any security in the immediate area. I knew I was fucked.

"Rolanda, what are you doing here?" Jessica asked surprised.

"What the fuck you mean what am I doing here? What are you doing here with the town slut in a private room?" the girlfriend, now known as Rolanda, spat.

"I'm not the town's slut, you got me fucked up." I couldn't fight, but I wasn't gonna be disrespected by a fat ugly bitch.

"Chill, please. We didn't do shit but talk," Jessica pleaded with her purple-haired Oompa Loompa.

"Let me up outta this hallway. Your problem is with her, not me," I advised.

"You're right, gone through," she agreed, shockingly.

"Ugly hoe," I mumbled under my breath.

Whap!

She slapped me in the right jaw from behind, followed up by pulling my hair until I was laid on the ground. I tried to fight back, but I was in a compromising position, being that I had no idea she was gonna hit me. Once she got on top of me, she punched me in the face so many times, I'd lost count. It wasn't until another one of the dancers came out that the fight stopped. The fucked-up part was, Jessica didn't attempt to stop her.

"Jessica, why didn't you stop her?" I asked as she walked in front of me to get to the security guard who had her girlfriend.

"Bitch please, stop my old lady? You got the game fucked up," she laughed.

"You are fucking evil! Do you see what she did to my face? This is how I make my money. I'm gonna press charges on you hoes," I yelled.

"You can't press charges on people you don't have information on, dummy," she responded to me as if she hadn't just poured her heart out to me. "It was all an act, stupid," she spat as if she'd read my mind. Now I understood why she never touched me nor allowed me any physical contact before kissing her forehead.

"Who sent you at me? You at least owe me that," I summoned for answers.

"If you fucking that many niggas to not know whose wife or girlfriend was coming for you, maybe you should retire that stank ass pussy. I almost died trying to complete this mission," she laughed and made a dash to the exit.

Chapter Four
"I'm A Nice Guy, But I Like To Walk On The Wild Side"
Wyatt "Snow" O'Sullivan

A fter spending time with Dominique last week, I really liked her style. I figured she would be a bratty chick because of the way she dressed in comparison to the rest of the girls on payroll at the club. They tried hard to look like money whereas she smelled like it and carried herself as such. She had a walk that would make a dude like me clean out his trust fund.

I was born Wyatt Joshua O'Sullivan. Both my parents are Irish, literally born in Ireland. They moved to New York when they found out I was baking in the oven. When people heard their accent versus mine, they would flip the fuck out. I had a straight New York accent and they'd wonder how, being that I was with them all of my life. Honestly, it was because I'd catch the ferry to Queens three days a week just to feel at home with the neighborhood kids. I felt out of place on the island, it was filled with privileged rich kids.

The crew in Queens would have rap battles and I would make beats for them. We were Black, White, Hispanic, and Muslim kids chasing a dream. In those days we referred to ourselves as the M.I.S.F.I.T.S., MF's for short. The acronym stood for Making It Selflessly, Fortunate In The Streets. We believed that as long as we had each other's backs, we could conquer the world.

That group was where I met Spencer, we were friends a very long time. That was, until he fucked my baby sister. True she gave it up to him, but he had ill intentions. Plus, I wouldn't have done that kind of fuck shit to him or any of our homeboys. We were thick as thieves back in those days, it was good times.

Leaving New York when I was twenty-one, I'd learn to shoot my shot on my own. My parents told me that I had four years after high school to prove to them that I could create tracks, sell dope beats, and produce music. People in the rap industry took me for a joke because I was a tatted-up white boy from Centre Island. The RnB industry wouldn't give me a chance because I didn't look the part, so to speak.

I knew the music in my heart and soul belonged on wax and it wasn't the genre the world assumed I should be in. Here I was years later, in the same city with my teen rival, checking for his woman. Karma had a way of playing out in the good guy's favor.

The dancers at Purple Haze called me White Chocolate. It was the typical nickname for a white boy that hung with black dudes and I really wasn't feeling it. I had never attempted to be anyone other than myself. I listened to a lot of Rap and R&B because it's what I vibe with, not because I was trying to be black. What the hell was *trying to be black* anyway? I wasn't into hard rock, country, techno, nor did I like pop; until I found out that was the genre that Michal Jackson and Prince dominated.

When I first moved to Baton Rouge, I felt at home. People looked at me as a person, not as a white boy. When I tried my hand in the music business in upstate New York, the first question from any artist was, *What you know about this industry, white boy?* Saying that the question pissed me off, didn't scratch the surface of how I truly felt. Here in Big Raggedy, all they cared about was a motherfucker producing fire ass beats, so they could lay down their tracks. After I got here, I started an Instagram page with samples of beats and promotions for whoever to contact me for more. Before I knew it I'd had several artists to reach out. Unfortunately, it wasn't working fast enough to pay my bills, which led me to where I am today.

"White Chocolate, they in there fighting like crazy and I ain't tryna get into that shit," Ja'Monica said as she casually walked up to me. She stood there patting her weave like a hood-rat.

"Who? Where are they fighting at?" I asked the stripper whose stage name was Chastity. Wasn't shit pure about her ass. Nonetheless, her name suggested so. I shook my head at the thought of how many nights I'd seen her in and out of the Purple Room. If anything tripped me out about a stripper, I guess it would be the names, they were farfetched.

"White Chocolate you sexy as fuck, yeah boy. You should let me suck your dick one night," she said suggestively.

"Girl, you could never suck my dick. Where is the fight?" I responded with my lip curled in disgust.

"Oh I ain't good enough to give you a bj, you think I'm beneath you? I know your secret, you fucking trust fund kid. Yeah, I know all about you, upstate New York raised, Ireland made," she laughed as if it were a secret.

Sure, I didn't share my background with people because I didn't want to be judged. But damn, how the fuck did she know. Somebody had to be pillow talking. People seemed to assume you were weak if you came from money.

"Where's the fucking fight, Ja'Monica Pierre?" I blew out an exasperated breath. "Aren't you from Pierre Part? Don't your family own half of everything in Pierre Part?" her eyes bucked from her head like the cartoons. "Oh, I know shit, too. Why are you out here fucking for a buck when you are a trust fund kid just like me? Your family's money is much longer than mine."

Kissing her teeth and rolling her eyes, she finally told me that the fight was in the locker room. Once I made it there, the locker room was in complete disarray. It looked like there was a melee in that bitch and it was obvious who the scrappers were. There was titties and hair weaves everywhere.

As soon as I opened my mouth to get information for C-Note, he busted into the locker room. "Angelic and Diamond, you two bitches is fired. It's always y'all and

I'm losing money because of this shit. Everyone in here know I tolerate a lot, but this is the fourth fight between y'all in six weeks. Get ya shit and get the fuck outta my establishment," he yelled. "Snow, get the cleaning crew to come through here and get my shit nice and fresh again," he commanded.

It was Thursday night and the shits was already getting started. I swear I ain't ready for the weekend. Ok, maybe I was. Dominique only worked on Friday and Saturday nights. She was the best dancer in the building. She danced with so much poise and grace. I'd shot her a couple of text messages, but being the fella I am, I respected the fact that she had a man and couldn't always respond.

As the night came to an end, I was locking up the doors and received a text message.

Dommie: Hey, meet me at Denny's.
Message read 02:10
Me: Woman, that's in Metarie. Are you serious?
Message sent 02:11
Dommie: Yep. Are you coming or nah?
Message read: 02:11
Me: Yeah, I'll be there in about 30...
Message sent 02:12

Bruh, this woman is tripping, inviting me to breakfast during booty-call hours. Then a thirty-minute drive from the club. *What the hell is she doing in Metarie anyway?* I thought as I got into my car and headed to the location. Hitting the start button on my blacked-out 2016 Chevy Camaro, the music blared through the surround sound Kenwood speakers I had installed. Of all the brands that had come along through the years, I still chose Kenwood.

"Yeah I'm tryna make you mine. Put a tingle in your spine. We got to vibe, we got a wave. You should ride on it, All the places I could take you girl is limitless," Usher crooned the lyrics to his hit *No Limit*. That song was clever. I like the fact that he tapped into his New Orleans accent during some of the verses. That shit was bomb as fuck.

After listening to a few more tracks on the *Hard II Love* album, I had arrived at my destination. I couldn't believe all it took was her asking me to meet her and I went. I haven't even kissed her pretty ass lips and was already doing crazy shit. Exiting my vehicle, I decided to pull my security shirt off and roll with the white tee that I'd worn underneath.

I walked in and noticed her sitting at the rear, near a window.

"Welcome to Denny's. Will you be dining alone?" The blonde-haired blue-eyed hostess asked as she looked on seductively.

"Nah, I'm meeting my girl here. Matter of fact, she's right there."

I left her standing there with her mouth hanging open. Dominique didn't notice me until I was damn near to the table. With her head down in her phone the whole time, I wondered what had her attention. However, when she did take notice, she slid her phone into her Celine bag and stood to give me a hug.

She wore a black see-through shirt with a sequined bra underneath, paired with boyfriend jeans with slits in them, and a pair of sequined peep-toe Louboutin heels. Baby was nice. She had my manhood wanting to make himself present. What she had in them jeans had my mufuckin' mind hectic.

"What's up, Wyatt? You looking at me like I'm a snack or something," she smiled.

"Nah, I wouldn't disrespect you like that, boo. You the full course, and since I can't have you, you all meat and I'm a vegetarian." My steel grey eyes bored into her.

"You're so damn corny," she laughed. "But, I gotta give it to you, that was cute," she smiled.

We laughed at my expense for a moment. It was nice to see her smile, in the almost year and a half that she'd been at the club, she was reserved. The only people I'd seen her interact with was Sharae, C-Note, and the barmaid, Arronisha. I understood her reason behind only associating with a handful of people. It was to avoid shit like what popped off between the two girls tonight. Arronisha was good people, her heart exuded through her smile. All the dancers rocked with her because of that reason alone.

"So, what are you doing out here in the city this time of morning?" I inquired.

"Honestly?" she quizzed.

"I asked, didn't I woman?" I responded. I had a feeling some sad ass shit was about to leave her beautifully decorated lips. It was cool how she had the moon setting on the water in her lipstick. It looked like airbrush or something.

"I dropped Spencer off at the airport last weekend to take care of some business in Tennessee. I was supposed to pick him up at 12:05. He texted me at 12:30 telling me he had to stay an extra few days, but I was already waiting at the gate. He came out and jumped into the driver's seat of Latrice's car," she stated as her eyes welled up.

"Who is Latrice?" was the only question that came to my nonchalant mind.

"Sharae, my ex-best friend." The dam broke. "I'm sorry. I didn't call you here to talk about that. It makes me sad to know that they both hate me so much."

"Nah, they hate themselves and project it on you, love. Don't ever let anyone deflect their misery onto you. When you look in the mirror, are you happy?"

"No," she cracked. I almost got up to console her, but I refrained from doing so. "I want to be happy, but it's like love is not on my side. Every time I'm near the doorstep of love, it shuts me out," she wept silently as I looked on in anguish.

"Do you love him or are you complacent? If it's the latter, the only way you'll get away from that situation is to love yourself more." Honesty was the only way I saw to get through to her at that point. If she wasn't tired of it, there was nothing that I could do to help her.

After sitting for a while, we decided to make a morning of our outing. The sun was coming up and I took her to one of my favorite spots in the city, to watch the sunrise. Luckily for the both of us, she had a blanket in her car. Watching her nipples grow hard against the windchill coming off the river, was a challenge for me.

Bit by bit she was opening up to me, I had no idea what God's plan was. All I knew for a fact was that I was onboard with the process. However it played out, it played out. I, however, had one reserve. I wanted to let her know that I knew Spencer from back in the day. I didn't want her to think it was some kind of gameplay of revenge. All I needed was for him to throw salt as he'd done so many times before. He'd gotten to some of the MF's, the others knew him for what he was, a selfish son of a bitch.

At this point in our friendship building, I didn't see a need to expose my hand. I'd wait to see where this goes.

Chapter Five
"If They With Me, Just Know They With It, And They Bout It"
Lestlee

I had made it through high school and out of Baton Rouge. I hated that country ass place, it was a dead-end for anyone with a dream. Especially if you were black. I went to Istrouma High where every female either came in pregnant or left pregnant. That fuckin' neighborhood was the worst. My sister had made enough money to move us out the hood, but I begged to finish high school there because I had high chances of receiving a scholarship.

Those hoes weren't only dumb enough to get pregnant when they couldn't work, but also dumb enough to not graduate. Silly asses. I guess it was a generational curse. My mother got pregnant with Tricey her ninth grade year, her friends all had kids the same year or the following one. When Tricey was sixteen, she got pregnant. She thought I didn't know that she had an abortion so, I kept it that way.

One day her and mama was arguing, they assumed I was asleep in my bedroom. I heard mama tell her that she was dumb for killing her baby. Then Tricey told her she was dumb for keeping us and turning her into a whore because she didn't know the first thing about parenting. After that it was like a rumble in the Bronx. Tricey had been fighting mama back since she was thirteen.

I remember one day when I was thirteen, mama said that her friend had come over to meet me. I was headed downstairs in a cat suit that she had made me put on, Tricey ran out of her room to stop me.

"Go back to your room, now," Tricey yelled.

"Mama wants me to meet Freddy," I stated with an attitude. She always thought she was running things.

"Lee, go to your muthafuckin' room before I knock your head off your shoulders," she gritted through closed teeth and tight lips.

Mama grabbed me by my arm and snatched me towards the wall where she stood. "You don't tell my child what the fuck to do. I pushed her out of my pussy and if I want her to meet my friend she will meet my damn friend." Mama got into Tricey's face.

"If you introduced Lee to Freddy like you introduced me to Bruce, I promise you BRPD will be carting me off to prison and both of y'all bodies will be in the morgue at Baton Rouge General." Tricey looked mama square in the eye and never flinched.

"Take her punk ass. He didn't want a virgin anyway, I was trying to save the miles on your pussy," Mama told her. Tricey slapped the hell outta mama that day. I don't know if it was the threat of Tricey killing her or if mama felt slighted, but she didn't hit her back.

Once mama got back to the living room, Freddy beat her ass to sleep. Every blow was followed by yelling. He fussed that she used all of his dope on a promise of my virginity and he didn't get it. Once he finished beating her ass, he headed towards us. Tricey pushed me into the room and told me to lock the door.

"Look Freddy, if you want to be filled with a hot six, take one more muthafuckin' step. If you wanna live to smoke another piece of crack, shoot up some more heroin, or whatever the fuck you do; take the L and walk the fuck away," she paused. My breathing became silent, I had no idea what was going on out there.

I heard footsteps, glass breaking, then a momentary silence.

Knock. Knock. "Open the door Lee," I was relieved to hear Tricey's voice. "He left but not before breaking all the picture frames and vases on the way out," she laughed but I was still afraid.

"Lestlee. Lestlee, girl do you hear me talking to you? What the hell are you thinking about?" My roommate Neekie asked once I snapped back to reality.

"Girl, I zoned out thinking about Jonnel's fine ass. He know he put that work on me last night," I lied.

"You done lost your virginity and are just wilding the fuck out, ain't you?" she curled her lip.

I wanted to smack the fuck outta her for testing my gangster. However, the truth was, I'd shone myself in that light by lying on my pussy. Not wanting to give anyone my sex besides Spence, I had been pretending to be boo'd up with other guys. I didn't allow anyone a slice of Spence's pie because I only craved him. Had he not set ground rules for me the night I lost my virginity, I would've transferred from The U to Southern University to make myself available to him.

"Look, are we going to The Tavern or nah? It's the weekend and I ain't trying to hear that bullshit you talking. I'm trying to turn up." Hoping I would find someone to catch my interest, I played along with her accusation.

"Nah. I was thinking we should go to Hooligan's, we are always at The Tavern. Hooligan's may have guys from Florida International, you know I don't like these hood niggas at The U." Neekie kissed her teeth.

Funny thing about Nekiya, she talked about hood niggas, but she was from the roughest streets that Chicago had to offer. The mere area of Riverdale topped the crime rate in Baton Rouge by a landslide. That's a big pill to swallow. I guess she was leaning towards the saying, *Being from the environment doesn't mean that you must be of the environment?*

"Bitch, you funny. That's cool, we can go to the beach if you want to. I just wanna get out of here. We been held up in here for the first half of the semester, it's midterms and I need to get out of my own head," I smiled. I genuinely meant that.

"You make me so damn sick," she said as she laughed.

"What I do??" I replied.

"Always worried about quizzes and midterms! You're one of the most intelligent people I know. Book-wise anyway." Neekie shouldered me and I laughed at her dig about my assumed promiscuity. "You can sleep on your notes and pass the exam. What time are we leaving?"

"My bad, suge. I guess my sister made me study so much, I've formed the habit of paying extra attention so that I wouldn't need as much study time."

Bzzz. Bzzz. Bzzz.

My cellphone vibrated against the coffee table. "Shit. I forgot to respond to Tricey earlier. I know she's cussing me out some bad," I said to no one in particular.

Making it to my phone, I notice that the number was unknown. I picked it up to open the message.

225-993-2220: Hey beautiful, what's been up?
Message received 19:56

Me: Who is this?
Message sent 19:58

I was looking at my phone wondering who was hitting my line and how they'd gotten my number. It was odd for that to happen since their number wasn't saved in my contacts.

225-993-2220: Fuck you mean who is this?
Message received 20:01

I didn't have to play the guessing game with an unknown asshole. I was not about to go back and forth. What I was about to do was get ready to hit the scene with my girls and possibly find me a man.

Ignoring the childish shit, I went into my room. We lived in an off-campus apartment, not far from the college. I started to search for something to wear to the club. I pulled everything out of my closet, and I own a lot of threads. Being that I was a fashion design major, I was big into vintage pieces. Settling on a black catsuit, I paired it with a burgundy and tan long-sleeved button-down shirt and a pair of tan Mary Jane shoes. My sew-in was fresh so all I had to do was shower and get dressed.

By the time we were dressed and ready, it was after 11 o'clock. We headed downstairs and hopped into her Audi. I noticed the notification light flashing on my iPhone. Deciding to take a peek, I slid the bar and noticed I had several messages. All of them were from the unknown number that had texted me earlier in the evening. I started to delete the whole thread but curiosity got the best of me, so I slid the bar and opened the thread.

225-993-2220: So you just gone ignore a nigga huh?
Message received 20:29

225-993-2220: If you busy, say you fuckin busy instead of being childish.
Message received 21:53

225-993-2220: Dam lil' baby, you gave a nigga the v-card and now you doing me jurty? That's what's up, I'mma leave you alone boo. Do yo thang love 100.
Message received 22:46

That last message made me feel a sensation in my thighs. Just remembering the night Spencer took my virginity, made my pussy thump in anticipation of the next time we would link up. Deciding to finally text him back, I smiled so bright that the inside of the car lit up.

Me: oh, so you talkin to me now? How did you get my number?

Message sent 23:47

"Ugh, who's texting you lil' nasty?" Neekie asked nosily.

"Don't worry about my pussy, just make sure we get to the club safely," I laughed and leaned my back against the door of the car, so she wouldn't look in my message screen.

"You do realize I can see your whole message reflect through the window?" she laughed.

225-993-2220: Look, I'm in Miami. I want that pussy in my room in an hour.

Message received 00:13

Chapter Six
"High Off Of Promises and Drunk Off of Dreams"
Dominique

H ow's life treating my favorite daughter these days?" My mother asked. Her voice and tone was always so genuine. I wondered how she kept a leveled head all of the years she'd been with my father.

"It's fair. I guess," I responded nonchalantly. I didn't want to alarm them of the fight Spencer and I had before meeting them here. Sure, I had make-up caked on my face to hide the redness of where he'd slapped me. I still couldn't believe he attacked *me* for telling *him* that *he'd* given *me* Gonorrhea. I couldn't fathom his logic. The nerve of him, tuh!

"What do you mean by that, princess? You should never have to guess about anything in your life, it should be cut and dry," my dad butted in. I couldn't tell him what I was going through, he'd never understand. He loved my mother so much it hurt to watch. Even after all the years had come and gone, the love, lust, and adoration was ever-present in his eyes.

"Maybe it has something to do with the reason you have your face covered in foundation," my mother pointed out. My complexion flushed in embarrassment, I couldn't believe she had taken notice.

"Mom!" I gritted.

"What the hell is going on with you and that no good yank?" my dad queried. He'd finally voiced his disdain for Spencer. He usually held his tongue on our relationship, but it's been evident that he didn't care for him since day one.

"Dad!" I gasped.

"Well, I'll lay this out on the table for you, Nique," mom paused. "We've noticed every bruise, every hair out of place, and every scratch. We were waiting on you to ask for help or mention it, but you never have. We decided that if you didn't say anything today, we would point it out."

"You have?" Tears began to fall. I couldn't believe that they'd been holding out this long on my not-so-secretive abusive relationship.

"Do you want to come home?" Mom queried.

"No ma'am. That is my place, he has to leave," I rebutted.

"Baby, you don't have to put up with that bullshit ass motherfucker. I will kick his monkey-ass if you want me to," my dad hugged me and I cried even harder.

After all was said and done, I headed home with a new attitude. I'd been over Spence's shit for a while but now, I had a new strength. I was no longer taking any shit from him, whatever he'd give me, I would give it back to him. It was time I become a new woman.

On my way to the house, I tuned into Jazmine Sullivan's *Forever Don't Last* and got in my feelings. I felt it in my soul when she said *I think of the pain and I realize that I belong by myself*...in that moment, I decided to take my life back.

Pulling under the awning for covered parking, I took notice of Spencer's white Toyota Tundra. He talked a lot about balling, but he drove a damn Toyota, tuh. Just the sight of his truck made me curl my lip. Not wanting to deal with him, I was hoping he'd be gone as he usually was when I returned from meeting my parents.

After walking inside, I took notice to how he'd left everything he'd touched strewn about. It had been two hours since I'd left, and he'd managed to cook a full meal for himself, drink a six pack of Bud Light long necks, and eat chips and dip. What pissed me off the most was the simple fact that he'd left his trash everywhere. The least the bastard could've done was made enough food for me since he left the fucking mess for me to clean.

Busting into the door of the master's bedroom with fire in my eyes, Spencer's raggedy-ass was stretched across my queen-sized bed in his boxer shorts. I stood over him with hatred in my heart. Before today, no matter how bad it was between us, seeing him depleted any ill feelings I harbored.

Upon approaching him, I noticed he had hickies all over his chest. They lined his collarbone like a gold chain. Whoever he was fucking was in blissful passion. That nigga didn't allow me to put passion marks on him and here he's laying in my bed full of them. "Oh hell naw, this nigga just didn't. I know he's fuckin' lying to me," I spoke aloud.

"I'm 'bout to stab his ass up, this muthafucka taking me for a joke!" I yelled as I headed to the kitchen. Once I entered the kitchen I grabbed several knives from the butcher's block and headed back down the hallway. I talked to myself all the way to my bedroom.

Upon making it to the room door, my eye started to twitch. I knew if I had stabbed his ass the way I wanted to, I would've ended up in prison for a very long time. I contemplated whether it was worth serving time over his abusive, cheating, dog-ass. Deciding against it, I walked back into the kitchen and grabbed the largest pot I owned. I filled it to the brim with ice water and smiled devilishly.

No sooner than I made it to the bed, he was rubbing his womanizing dick and smiling in his sleep. I guess he was dreaming about the bitch that put the passion marks on his body. I stood over him and poured every ounce of water there was over his chest and groin area.

"Bitch!" he gritted as he laid there temporarily paralyzed. "I'm 'bout to fuck you up!"

"Fuck you! I fuckin' hate you, all you do is cheat!" I responded.

"If you knew how to fuckin' please a nigga, you would be enough."

"That reflects on the teacher, bitch! You taught me everything I know, so whatever I don't know that's on yo fuck-ass, tuh!" I slammed the pot on his stomach causing him to grunt in pain.

He stood to his feet looking like a fish out of water and I'd had enough of seeing him. I attacked him like a rabid dog; scratching, punching, and yelling every obscenity I knew. We fell onto the bed and I promise I was scrapping like Mike Tyson. He eventually rolled me over after coming out of his daze from the flurry I had put on his ass.

"What the fuck is wrong with your crazy ass, Dominique?" The nerve of him to ask me that question.

Laughing hysterically, he looked at me as if I had lost my damn mind. Honestly, I had. He was slowly diminishing my sanity. The longer I stayed in this toxic relationship, the more I was losing myself. In that moment, the infamous words of my nanny rang in my head. *What you allow, is what will continue.* I had zoned out completely.

Slap, slap, slap!

He slapped me several times across the face. "Oh no bitch, you not about to pretend to have blacked-out. Snapback so you'll be aware of this ass-whooping. You gone respect that I am a man with needs that you ain't fulfilling and I'mma do what the fuck I have to, to keep my needs met," he slapped me again.

I tried rolling him off of me, however he was too heavy. He had no idea that I was a scrapper, though. I'd been submissive and accepting the ass-whippings that he'd been handing out regularly. Not today though, this shit was overkill. I was gonna give him what he gave me. I summoned the strength from all of my forefathers and flipped his ass off of me.

Taking notice of the shocked expression that his face held, I took advantage of the moment. I grabbed the wrought-iron newspaper holder next to my bed and lit into his ass. He was shocked, to say the least. Once the initial shock wore off, it was on like Donkey Kong inside of the bedroom. As with all of the other fights, I never yelled out for help. I had been taking the beatings in silence, therefore I would fight back as such.

We were going blow for blow until we were both tired of swinging. All of the talking he was doing was uncalled for because I wasn't listening. I'd tuned him out a long time ago. He took one final blow and I immediately felt my eye start to swell. The tears welled in my eyes, but I refused to allow him to see another one drop... ever again in life. He was no longer worthy of my joy, nor my pain.

Following the knock-down-drag-out, I was hungry as hell. After showering, I headed to the kitchen to cook steak with grits and eggs. I had taken the steak out to make dinner, but I refused to ever cook for him again. In the midst of me prepping the steak, he walked into the kitchen and rubbed my arm. Neither did I embrace nor reject his touch, I was numb.

It wasn't until he attempted to kiss the side of my face that I side-stepped him and looked at him crazily. Not once did I open my mouth to speak.

"Dominique, you want me to fuck your ass up some more?" he asked. I flipped my steak without saying a word. It was almost browned to perfection. "Why the fuck is there only one piece of steak in that muthafuckin' skillet?" Still, my lips were sealed. Other than eating my very delicious meal, I had no reason to part my swollen soup-coolers.

Turning to place the grits and eggs on my plate, I noticed a look of defeat on his handsome face. Sure, I felt crazy for still thinking he was handsome, but in that moment, I had won.

"So, you not gonna fuckin' answer me, bitch?" he growled.

As I placed the nice, hot, and juicy steak atop of my cheese grits, I looked him square in the eyes and smiled. "You know what, Spencer?" I asked rhetorically. "Every battle isn't worth a fight." With that, I walked off, bruised and battered, feeling a bit of redemption.

"Dominique, let me find out you got a nigga on the side and I'mma paralyze your ass. And that nigga... he good as dead," he talked more to himself.

I was so into my food that I was having a foodgasm. Ain't nobody got time for that.

"Ooooh, yummy! This fuckin' steak is the bomb, Dommie. You did that shit girl," I gave myself a vote of confidence on the food I was devouring. He looked at me as if I had lost my mind, and I had.

"You can't ignore me forever," he patted me on top of my head like I was his fucking pet. I knew what he was trying to do. I dare not allow him to ruffle my feathers. He attempted to lean in and kiss my cheek, but I jerked my neck so hard, I thought I had given myself whiplash.

"You know you want this dick. That's the problem, you ain't had none in a while. That's why you trippin'," he grabbed his package. "I'm leaving anyway."

With that he left. Finally, I had order and peace in my chaotic world. I'd come to the conclusion that I was done, I was over him and this relationship.

Chapter Seven
"If She Catch Me Cheating I Will Never Say I'm Sorry"
Spencer

I t's been a few days since I'd left Dominique's apartment. She'd lost her fuckin' mind thinking she could fight me and win. I had to hit her harder than usual, that bitch packed a mean-ass punch. Maybe if she would've fought me back the first time, rather than being weak and submissive, I would've never laid my hands on her again. As hard as she hit, I definitely would've thought twice about it.

I had been chillin' at my pad, alone. There was no way I would show up to Tricey's house with all the bruises I'd had on my face. On the real, I was more afraid of what she'd do if she saw the passion marks. Knowing that it was something Dominique and I weren't into, she would've been tight enough to go dumb on my ass, yo.

She didn't play that shit with me. I like that she knew how to be dominant and not emasculate me at the same time. Real talk, I liked that she was a freaky ass bitch that knew her worth as a woman. She came from the gutter and didn't allow anyone to run her mental the way spoiled-ass Dominique allowed me to pull her strings, being her puppet master. I was never into weak bitches, thanks to my mother.

The passion marks had finally faded out due to some home remedies I'd learned back in Queens. When I was thirteen, I used to meet up with girls my age at the bodega, buy them hot Cheetos, and fuck the dog shit outta them. Back then, all pussy was good pussy, so it was passion marks for everyone. When they'd go inside of the bodega they'd come out with rat-tailed combs, combing the passion marks out. They said that broke up the pocket of blood that I'd sucked into the spot and once they got home they'd nurse it with a cold spoon. That's what I'd done, now I was passion mark free.

> **MGP:** Where are you?
> *Message sent 19:06*
> **Me:** What's good shawty?
> *Message sent 19:08*
> **MGP:** Don't what's good shawty me. Where yo ass at nigga?
> *Message sent 19:08*
> **Me:** I'm at home. Where you at?
> *Message sent 19:10*

I knew some shit was about to pop off because of how she was checking me through text. I had literally gotten my ass handed to me by Dom, I didn't feel like fucking with all these crazy ass hoes. I missed my lil' baby.

> **MGP:** Get your ass over here NOW. This pussy needs attention.
> *Message sent 19:11*

Lestlee must've done a number on me because I really didn't feel like fuckin' Latrice today. All I had been thinking about was getting back to Miami. However, I couldn't tell her no because that would've brought on a barrage of questions that I didn't wanna answer. It was either that, or Dominique had my head gone. Even after days had passed, she still hadn't called to check on me or crying for me to come back home. I guess she'd finally meant what she'd said.

I snatched up my keys, hit the alarm code, and walked out. After I hopped in my car, I tuned into Post Malone's newest album and turned up the volume. That boy was a beast, he topped charts and was still climbing. He reminded of my homie Wyatt and if I'm honest, it's probably why I fuck with Post so tough.

Before long, I was pulling into the driveway of my side bitch's house. Walking up to the door, she pulled it open before I was able to ring the bell. Proud of the sight before me, my dick stood to attention. My shit was harder than steel-toed boots and I was ready to fuck her ass to sleep.

She grabbed my shirt and pulled me into a long kiss. She worked her tongue like a professional trying to win the top position in my life. All I could do was grab her ass and indulge in the tongue fight we had going on. As if on cue, *Permission* by Ro James blared through the Pink Pill that I had purchased for her a few months ago.

She grabbed my wood through my grey joggers and dropped to her knees. Mind you, I was still standing in the doorway. Bitch was 'bout to give her neighbors a show. If she didn't mind letting them see her go to work, who was I to contest it? That's what the fuck I meant about her having no inhibitions. She didn't give a damn and would please me in any setting.

I grabbed the back of her head and enjoyed the ride on the way to ecstasy. After sending my unborn kids down her throat, she got up and wiped the corners of her mouth. "Are you hungry, boo?" she asked as she walked into the kitchen.

If I could change anything about her, it would be how she didn't clean up after we had sex. Whether it was oral or intercourse, Dom cleaned up immediately.

"Nah. I was just finishing my food when you texted me," I lied like a champion. I hadn't eaten since breakfast.

"I bet you did. Anyways, I'm boutta eat before we finish what I started. Where you been hiding at?"

"Hiding? That's one thing I don't do. You got the game fucked up, yo," I said with a mug on my face and a boot in my grill.

"It's merely a figure of speech. Talking reckless gone get you fucked up. Don't come in my house getting jazzy with me like you stupid," she responded.

"My bad, yo," I gritted my teeth. I was getting sick of her trying me.

"Anyways, Lee done fell in love with one of them lil' fuck boys out there in Miami," she broke the ice.

"Is that right?" I tried to sound unbothered and uneducated by that admission. I didn't want to set off her antennas that the person she was diggin' was me.

"Yep, she said he broke her virginity and they had only had sex twice. But she seems quite smitten over him. I told her I wanted to meet his ass, but she is refusing."

"Is that right?" I smiled knowing she was speaking highly about me.

"Yep, she's saying that she doesn't know how serious they are, so she ain't ready to introduce him," she slowed her words. "What you smiling bout?" she asked.

"I ain't smiling," I responded.

"But you were, you may not be now. Is there something I should be worried about?" she queried.

"Nah, I was really amused because Dominique fuck ass finally tried to fight me back. That bitch got hands. I almost forgot I was fighting a girl."

"Well, you sitting up here smiling about a bitch while I'm talking to you about my sister. That's flake as fuck. Nigga, you foul," she fumed.

"My bad, bae. Don't be mad at a nigga. I heard everything you said about your lil' sis. Respect her wish and let her introduce her pissy dick lil' boyfriend on her time. Was he a virgin, too?" I questioned, pretending not to know what had happened.

"You know, you're right. I'mma let it be. On another note, Nique got them hands. That bitch had to fight throughout our middle and high school years. You know she is a trust fund kid and bitches would pick on her every chance they got. One day she beat up two chicks and their brother for fucking with us," she smiled in a moment of reminiscing.

"Where were you?" I asked with my eyebrow raised.

"Standing on the side, duh?" she put her hand out and scarfed down another spoon of jambalaya.

"What you mean? You stood in the shadows and watched her fight three people?" I asked in shock.

"Well, yeah. I can't fight so what else was I supposed to do?" she admitted.

"Wow," was all I could say at the moment.

"Wow?" she huffed. "What the fuck is that supposed to mean?"

"I'm just saying, you're pretty damn bossy to say you don't have any dogs to back it up," I laughed. "Why haven't you ever said anything?" I questioned.

"About her knowing how to fight or me not knowing how? Either way, I didn't think it was relevant. So she fucked your ass up, huh?" she laughed. "It's about time your bitch finally stood up to your ass. Now, that's sexy as fuck, love. Hearing that got my pussy leaking. You ready to fuck me?" she asked as she sat her plate in the sink and walked toward the bedroom.

I followed like a lovesick puppy. Although I was pissed about the revelation, she'd just gotten me horny by calling my girl sexy in my presence. I'mma talk her into a threesome soon. I was down for the *my girl got a girlfriend* type shit. What man wasn't? Nah, mean?

She popped a sexy lady and handed me one with a bottle of water. Before long we were both humping like rabbits. Ecstasy pills had a way of making a man's stroke game and a woman's level of horniness endless. It was on like the HOT sign at Krispy Kreme's, all damn night.

The next morning had come and I stood in the mirror looking at my eyes. The whites were off-white, but I assumed it was the fact that we'd been up fuckin' all night and half the morning.

Tricey walked in the bathroom and farted so loud it made my stomach turn. The smell that followed was atrocious. "Look, if you have to shit just say that. I don't do the shit and talk thing."

"You can get out," she kissed her teeth. "I gotta talk to you before you leave, though." Following that bit of information, was another fart. She curled her lip and rolled her eyes as if I was the culprit.

If I could change anything about Tricey, it would be her tact. She was just too damn ghetto. I headed to the kitchen thinking she had made a nigga breakfast. We had a lot of sex over the past eight hours. "Who was I kidding?" I said to myself.

"The fuck you thought? You couldn't have been thinking I had cooked, tuh! You got your bitches mixed up," she laughed as she sat at the table. I didn't even know she had finished in the bathroom. As fast as she made it in here behind me, she couldn't have taken care of much hygiene besides wiping her ass.

"That was fast," I said in reference to her taking a shit.

"Yeah. Anyways, I'm pregnant and it's yours."

"The fuck? How you figure you pregnant and how you know it's mine?" I rebutted, not feeling how she just dropped that shit on a nigga's table.

"The fuck you mean? Don't try to play me like I'm some two-dollar hoe, Spence. You know we been fucking like crazy without condoms."

"Nah son. We been using condoms, I strap up every fuckin time," I said looking at her crazy. "Ain't no way. And I thought you did the Morning After pill thing when we had sex."

"Nope, those middle of the night sessions, you don't use condoms. I wake up with my pussy wet and hop on that dick. The fuck you think, I wanted this shit. Have a baby by a nigga that half-ass hustle. Nigga you ain't shit. The only reason I fucked you was to get back at Nique But then I found out the dick was good, so I been getting it on the regular."

"Is that right?" I laughed.

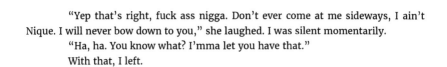

"Yep that's right, fuck ass nigga. Don't ever come at me sideways, I ain't Nique. I will never bow down to you," she laughed. I was silent momentarily.

"Ha, ha. You know what? I'mma let you have that."

With that, I left.

Chapter Eight
"My Skeletons, His Sins"
Latrice

I couldn't believe Spence tried me the way he did. He was bitch-made, and for him to ask me how I knew I was pregnant by him, was frivolous. First of all nigga, you ain't *that* dude. It's not like I want to be pregnant by a nothing ass fuck-boy, tuh. Second of all, I couldn't get pregnant if God falsely inseminated me because I had no uterus. It was stripped from me when I was eighteen. It was causing me more harm than good, being that I had been sexually active for so many years.

The less he knew, the better. I was set up to suck Nique dry. Spence had been wanting a baby for many years now. It was too many to count, but because of everything he'd put Nique through, she was not on board with giving him a child. With all of that, I had him eating right out of my hands. He did have to know that I wasn't pregnant, and I hoped he didn't bitch up and tell Nique, because my cover would sure enough be blown.

After popping all these new pills they had given me down at the Health Unit, the main ones being to treat my ailment, I decided to shower and get dressed. After work tonight, I was gonna hook up with a few friends, eat me some pussy, and come back home to my lonely ass bed.

They suggested I slowed up on drinking and drugging, but with the news I'd received, I'd rather die happy than to die full of medicine that didn't guarantee life. Getting out of the shower, I put on a cute outfit that I had gotten from PINK and a pair of Nike slides, then headed to my car. Just as I put my hand on the door latch to open it and slide into the driver's seat, a car whipped up beside me.

"Bitch, you done fucked the wrong husband, hoe," a tall dark female with a gap in her teeth yelled from the driver's side. By the time she'd jumped out of her car, I had gotten into mine and peeled out.

"How the fuck did this bitch find my house?" I said aloud as I checked my rearview mirror to see if she was following me. I didn't see her in the distance as I made my way to Airline Highway from Jefferson Park Drive. I'm fucked up in the head because I had been fucking James Lett for a while and she was his wife. Sometimes we used protection, sometimes we didn't. Those nasty dick niggas wasn't my problem. Their infidelity was their wives' shit to deal with. But, since I couldn't fight, and their bitches kept coming out of the woodworks, the females definitely are becoming an issue for me.

Waiting behind a couple of cars to turn right at the light, I notice Lett's wife's car cruising past. I decided to stall by turning into the restaurant's parking lot.

Technically I wasn't due to work for another hour, so I had time to waste. I hopped out and went in. When I got to the counter, I ordered two turkey necks and an order of corn. Yes, I am a Louisiana girl and I'm proud of it. Only Boot Babies know what I'm talm bout when I say turkey necks and corn. Fuck with us.

After indulging in that, I went into their restroom and washed my hands before heading out. After a quick mirror check, I freed my teeth of the leftover turkey neck meat and headed out.

"Fuck my life," I mumbled as I stopped dead in my tracks. I peered around the corner at the lady who stood ordering crawfish. "Dammit, I got twenty-five minutes to get to work on time," I mumbled. "Fuck it, if I walk fast maybe she won't notice me," I took off to the door.

"Bye Sharae, see you soon!" John, the owner said as I exited. I didn't want to be rude, but I didn't want to get noticed. She was the bitch that had two-pieced my ass not too long ago. Her and her bitch staged a play on my money-hungry ass.

"Bye John," I said without facing him. Great thing about being a stripper, not many people knew your government name. Plus, I only went by Latrice or Tricey. The only way you knew me by Sharae was to be family or have went to school with me. I was safe. When I made it to my car, she hadn't even turned around.

Pulling into my spot at the club, I felt a wave of relief. I was finally out of the lion's den. So far, I had dodged two ass-whippings today. I just wanted to make some good money, dassit, dasall! I walked into the club and the atmosphere was cool and crisp. Stopping at the bar, I ordered a double shot of Hennessy, downed it, and headed to the dressing room. No sooner than I had closed my locker, Wyatt's fine ass walked in.

"Damn you sexy as fuck, you know that, white boy?" I smiled.

"Look, Alizé. I didn't come in here for flattery nor is this a social visit. C-Note wants to see you in his office," he said sternly.

"What for? I just got here," I responded childishly.

"Yo, on the real, I don't know. Why don't you stop flapping your trap with me and ask him when you get to his office," he handled me like a man should.

"You know you want this pussy," I said as I approached him.

"Nah son, I don't do hand-me-downs. Feel me?" he laughed in my face making me want to spit in his. "Pussy," I muttered.

"Maybe. Nevertheless, it's tighter than yours," he laughed even harder.

It was like I was walking the green mile, as I headed down the short hallway in the direction of C's office. I didn't have a chance to knock because as soon as I made it there, Thunder, his bottom stripper, walked out in tears. The look she gave me put fear in my heart.

"Get your ass in here. Have a seat," he stared at me in disgust.

"What's up, Note?"

"Don't what's up me. You know what the fuck is going on."

"If I did, I wouldn't be as confused as I am. What's up?" I shot back.

"What's this I hear about you having HIV?" Shockwaves traveled from my head to my toes. What the fuck was he talking about?

"What? Me? HIV? Nah, I ain't got no muthafuckin' HIV. These hoes done took hating to another level, huh? Did that bitch Thunder come in here lying on my pussy?" I rambled.

"Look I don't know what's going on, but I do know you won't be performing in here tonight or any other fuckin' night. I let you slide with handing out gonorrhea, but you will not be assigning death sentences on my watch or on my name," he shook his head. "Giving niggas the clap had already caused me to take a hit in my pockets; but giving niggas life without parole is gone hit my bank."

"You can't get rid of me over hearsay! I don't have no fuckin HIV, C-Note," I sashayed around the desk and dropped to my knees prepared to suck him off as I'd usually done when I got into trouble with him.

"Get the fuck up and get the fuck out. I won't embarrass you by having you escorted out. Pretend like you quit, and clean out your locker."

"What the fuck am I supposed to do? This is all I have. Please," I cried.

"I will let you stay tonight on three conditions," he looked at me for acknowledgment.

"What's that?" I kissed my teeth and stuck my hand out.

"You agree to stay out of the Purple Room and pack your shit at the end of the night," he said.

"What's the third condition?"

"Oh, I did say three didn't I? The third one is more of a long term offer to stay."

"Okay," I said leerily.

"If you wanna stay indefinitely, you will have to submit to a HIV test."

"Hell nawl. Not anywhere in America will a muthafucka ask you to do that."

"Well, that proves my point. So tonight will be your last night and security will be watching. If you try to enter the Purple Room, you will be escorted out of the building and off of the premises. Understood?"

"This shit ain't right, C-Note. A bitch is being shady because I fucked her man, that's all that is," I informed him.

"Well look, I have a business to run. Take it or leave it." Looking me in the eyes, I noticed that his face held more seriousness than I'd ever seen before. His demeanor spoke business and his poise said not to try him.

"I'll have all of my shit out after the club shuts down. This is some fucked up shit. I just sent my sister off to college," I stood to walk away.

"It's the game and how it's played. Kitty Kat's would hire you any day of the week cuz you a bad bitch, Alizé. I just can't in good faith allow you to stay here with you denying you have HIV but also refusing to prove it. Louisiana is a red state and I have the right to get rid of you without cause."

"I'm confused, what the fuck you telling me all this extra shit fa?" My eyes bore a hole through his chest. I wanted to kill him. He knew Kitty Kats was in Cajun Country, they wouldn't want my black ass on their main stage.

He laughed, "I'm telling you this because I know you 'bout your paper. Don't waste your money on a lawyer because you'll lose."

I walked out of his door without a word. Just before it closed I heard him say to himself that he was blessed to have dodged a bullet. I guess he was saying that because all I ever did was suck his dick. He had never penetrated me or any of the dancers that I know of. He would let us give him head on the regular. One time, Thunder and I took turns eating each other out and sucking his dick. I never understood why he didn't fuck us, but who was I to question it. I got six-hundred to suck his dick and a grand to have an oral threesome with him and whoever he chose.

Making it to the end of the night without anything popping off, I cleaned out my locker and headed out. I couldn't believe I had been working at this damn club since I was eighteen. I'm twenty-five now, seven fucking years and he lets me go over a rumor that may or may not be true. What kind of bullshit is that?

I said goodbye to my locker, had my final words with the security guards, then headed to my car. The car next to mine had music blaring through its speakers. The vehicle was out of place, I had never seen it before. However, as they backed out, the lyrics of the song were loud and clear. Jazmine Sullivan crooned through the speakers as she sang the words to her hit song *Bust The Windows Out Your Car*. I tuned in with the song just as loudly as she sang: *I must admit it helped a little bit, To think of how you'd feel when you saw it, I didn't know that I had that much strength, But I'm glad you see what happens when...* while throwing my hand in the air.

When I was right up on my car, I noticed the two driver's side tires were flattened. I ran around to the other side, the front tire was the only one flat on the passenger side. "Fuuuuuuuck," I yelled. These bitches knew that if they'd flattened all four, I would be able to get tires through my insurance due to malicious vandalism. These fuck ass hoes played the player.

I walked around my car with a flashlight to see if they had keyed my shit. I didn't notice any damages until I made a full circle. On the hood, they had dug into it, YOU HIV HAVING WHORE!

I swear I thought I could ride this wave until I couldn't anymore. I don't know what to do now that more people know than who I had told, which was no one.

Chapter Nine
"This Time I Swear I'm Through"
Dominique

Standing in the vanity area in my bedroom, I stared at my reflection. I couldn't take in the idea of my physical beauty being tarnished by the man I loved whole-heartedly. I had been so smitten with him that I'd been allowing him to diminish my self-esteem. As I looked over my face, where the bruises were fading away, a tear rolled down my cheek. I swiped it away just as fast as it had fallen.

When I turned my head towards my jewelry case, the heirloom that my granny gave to me on my eighteenth birthday sparkled at me. It was a beautiful gold necklace with a diamond pendant. My grandfather had given it to her when she was sixteen. It'd been in the family for seventy-one years. Something inside of me willed me to pick it up, so I did.

Following me picking it up, my granny's voice came to me as clear as day. "Neekie, you don't ever need validation from a man to know your worth. If he loves you, you'll know. He will always put you first and the only time he will hurt you is when you two are in the bed, making whoopie," she'd always giggle when she'd say that. My pawpaw, on the other hand, would disappear. I guess he didn't want me to look at him oddly when granny talked about sex.

I held the necklace up to my chest and smiled in the mirror. With my grandmother on my mind, I thought of the Katt Williams special where he'd said: *It's called self-esteem, it's esteem of your muthafuckin' self. Simple bitches!* He was right. They both were. How did I lose myself? I had allowed a man to make me feel that I wasn't worthy of anything more than the ass-whippings he'd been handing out on the regular.

After putting eyeliner on my barely-there eyebrows, I grabbed my purse and headed to the grocery store. Winn-Dixie had a buy one, get one on the meat and their canned goods were ten for ten this week. I hadn't shopped for groceries since Spencer left, nor had I been to work. I hopped into my car and decided to listen to my favorite gospel artist. Hitting number seven on the disc changer, I skipped to track number two. After the piano opened the floor, Smokie Norful's anointed voice blasted through the speakers, singing *I Need You Now*.

I had cried my last tear over a man that had done me nothing but harm throughout the years we'd been together. In that moment, I felt myself finding my way back to my path. God had always led me in the way He'd wanted me to go, however, I had veered off of that path some time ago. Don't misquote me, I had never given up on my Lord and Savior. Simply put, I had given up on myself.

Making it down Jefferson Highway in record time, I hung a right onto Perkins Road then another right into the marketplace's parking lot. I grabbed my grocery list and headed in to knock down my second chore of the day. After grabbing all of the boxed and canned goods, I headed to the perishables. I took meat, eggs, and milk and placed them into my cart. Deciding to treat myself to that new Magnum ice cream, I led the cart into the frozen section and ran into the one person I'd least expected.

"Well, look what the cat done dragged out of hiding. What's good, Unique?" Halo spoke as if we were friends.

"First of all, I wasn't hiding. I had a few personal issues to deal with. Secondly, my name is Dominique, Unique is my alter-ego."

"My bad, chick. No harm, no foul. Damn, you can calm down for real, for real," she laughed. "I haven't seen you in two weeks, I'm just surprised to see you in my neck of the woods, is all."

"I guess this is both of our area, I live right down the street. I had to get a few things together, so I took some personal time off," I responded.

"Really? I also live down the street. In The Reserve to be frank," she stated, and I tensed up. That was where I lived as well. I guess she may have lived on the other side of the complex because I had never noticed her.

Her face was etched in friendliness, whereas, I was still stand-offish. I didn't trust her. She had never said more than three words to me in our work environment. Her demeanor on the outside of the club was the total opposite of what it was under the purple and blue lights.

"I see you looking at me crazy, chick. I'm not the devil, ya know. I just don't really rock with bitches I don't rock with," I figured my quiet disposition had her thinking I didn't trust her. Truthfully, I didn't.

"Again, before today I never knew you to say anything more than *Unique, you're next*. Forgive me if I seem a bit edgy."

"Look, I'm not the selfish bitch that walks around Purple Haze. Just like you, I too have an alter-ego. Her name is Halo and that bitch is about two things: dominating the stage and getting money. I can see that you went through something. I'm also willing to bet that your community dick ass man and that fucked-up in the head, ex-best friend of yours is the ones behind your anguish," she gave me a sincere look.

"Listen," I sniffled. "I'm not comfortable sharing my personal life with you. Not that I'm being rude or anything like that, but since you know my ex-best friend, I'm sure you understand why. Thanks to her, I don't trust females. She ripped me off and continued to smile in my face as if she hadn't stolen my money." Halo's demeanor screamed that she knew the whole story, or that something much more was missing from my simple admission.

"Honestly, that's not all she's been up to lately. But that's not my business. What I will tell you is that, you are a beautiful woman and God didn't put you on earth to be anyone's punching bag," she stared at my eye.

"How did you kn–!"

"Look," she began to shake her head and step closer to me. "I was a victim of domestic violence. It's a long story. Just know that I don't wish the pain I went through on my worst enemy. That is a horrible reality to lie about and to live with," she encased me in a loving hug, a hug that I had no idea I needed. In that moment, I broke. I let all of my pent-up anger, stress, and secrets fall freely onto her shoulders as did hers fall onto mine.

When we broke from the hug, we both reached into our oversized designer bags, pulling out a travel size package of Kleenex as a peace offering. We shared a laugh at the identical thought. "Thank you," I held onto her hand an extra few seconds. "I really appreciate you sharing your experience with me."

"It was warranted, love. Sometimes, I don't know how I made it out, but I fall to my knees and thank God that I did," she squeeze my hand.

We released our embrace and went our separate ways. Before she could get out of earshot, I called out to her. "Hey, Halo," she turned around, her eyes held more tears of her own.

"Yeah?" she quizzed.

"If you ever wanna talk, I'm in apartment eleven-fifteen. Of course, you know my hours," I smiled.

"I'll stop by sometimes," she turned to walk away but stopped abruptly. "And uh, my name is Felicity," she winked at me.

A barrier had been broken between us. In that moment we'd bonded over a secret that over one hundred-ninety thousand households covered in smiles and make-up. Per the statistics, roughly twelve hundred of those victims end up dead due to their silence. At the rate Spencer was going with the beatings, I was on my way to death by his hands.

Standing in line, I told myself that forever didn't always last. This time was the last time and I was through with his dog-ass. I will reclaim my independence, my individualism, my womanhood. I am she and she is me. It's time I got back to her.

I made it back to my apartment, put my groceries away, and decided to head to Perkins Road to treat myself to lunch. I was craving a big-fat, fully-dressed shrimp po-boy from Parrain's Seafood. Two things that could never be stolen from me was my love for family and my taste for food. I liked to cook as well as serve drinks from my little at-home bar.

I listened to some good music, let my windows down, and appreciated nature in route. It was the most relaxed peaceful day that I'd had in a long time.

Walking into one of my favorite spots, I took notice of the yellow peonies. This place always screamed friendliness and welcome. Aside from the amazing seafood, I think it's the reason I enjoyed the place. Cruising toward my usual table, I noticed Desha; she was *my* waitress. Her bubbly personality matched the atmosphere. It didn't matter if the food was good or not, people like her kept the customers coming back.

Initially, I went in wanting a shrimp po-boy, but upon getting inside and seeing someone with the Catfish Perdu, I had surely changed my mind. I mean, who could resist deep-fried catfish smothered in crawfish étouffée?

No sooner than I sat down, Jimekia walked over with a glass of strawberry-lemonade. "What's up Nique? Desha said she would be right with you, love," she smiled warmly. Her smile was so beautiful that you couldn't help but to match it with a smile of your own.

"Thanks Suge. Can you get me an order of alligator started, because I did bring my appetite."

"Don't you always?" We laughed. "I'll get that out to you shortly, boo," she strutted off looking like a whole meal. I ain't nowhere near a lesbian, but the bitch was bad, she would give the customers at Purple Haze a run for their money. I smiled to myself and took a sip of the absolute best drink I'd had in a while.

My gator bites came to the table piping hot. "Hey D, what's good love?" Desha asked as she placed my plate in front of me.

"I'm good ma, just hungry as usual," I smiled.

"Aren't you always?" Desha accused.

"Hey, you sound like your damn niece."

"Nah, she sounds like me. I'm the aunty." We laughed. "What can I get for you today? Just when I think I know what you love, you try something else. I won't waste my time guessing."

"True, true. But yeah, let me try that Catfish Perdu, suge."

"Mmm-mmm, you won't be disappointed. I promise. If you don't like it, I'll make Mekia pay for your food, love," she laughed and headed towards the kitchen to place my order.

I was tearing the alligator up, it was scrumptious. In my own little world, I was doing the fat-lady dance. The food and drink was so good. Man, listen I don't care how skinny you are, we all have an inner fat girl and that bitch dances every time we feed her.

"For you, beautiful," a very familiar voice said as the tattooed hand held a peony in front of my face from behind me.

I kicked myself for always sitting with my back to the door. I couldn't see the patrons coming or going. It was kind of embarrassing because I had been avoiding him like the plague since he'd met me in Metairie. "Why thank you for being so generous with Parrain's floral arrangements, Wyatt."

"Hey, it was genuine. It's the thought that counts, right?" He stood there smiling. Damn, this guy was getting more and more handsome each time I saw him.

"What are you doing in this part of town, anyway? Don't you live in South Baton Rouge?" I quizzed.

"Can a brother get some good seafood?" Wyatt returned. "I see you keep looking around, am I intruding?" he put his hand on his chest.

"Nope, I'm solo," I raised my eyebrow. "You wanna join me or are you meeting someone?" I shot back. Secretly, I was hoping he would join me. However, I was also on edge about being seen in public with a white man.

"You want me to sit next to you or across from you?" He laughed before sitting opposite of me. "Loosen up, Dommie. I'm just a white boy trying to get a minute of your time," he winked and stuck his long tongue out. I felt it in my thighs, Jesus.

"Why do you call me that?" I asked.

"Because I think it fits you. I know you dominate people's hearts," Wyatt smiled, more to himself. He was so reserved and laid back, he reminded me of my father.

"Is that right?" I asked rhetorically.

"I mean, that dude Spencer used to be running up on you like a bloodhound," he grinned.

"Yeah, because he was a jealous-hearted dog-ass nigga that thought I was out here doing what he was doing. Then it was because I work at the club. Bitches like Sharae make it hard for women like me, to be viewed as a decent woman in the industry. I don't want to talk about them, how was your day today?"

"My day was blessed. I made some dope beats, recorded with a local for about three hours, and then I ran into a beautiful woman. It couldn't get any better than this for me, queen," he looked at me intently. This man believes in God and set me on the highest throne. I almost melted.

"Queen, huh?" was all I could say. I felt giddy in his presence. He always said the right words. Why couldn't Spencer feel that way about me and treat me how I deserved to be treated. I wish he had half the couth that Wyatt has.

"Don't act like you don't know what's good. Why you been avoiding me, woman?" He asked, addressing the elephant in the room.

"You do know I have a man, right? He may not be what's best for me, but I'm not a cheater. I don't really do casual conversation without direction with other men. I don't wanna lead them on as if I'm so jump-off bitch."

"Well, what are we doing now?" his face etched in confusion. "Are we not having pointless casual conversation, without direction?"

His New York accent was thick, but his words rolled with every bit of annunciation possible. I love a well-spoken man. Spencer was well-educated. He graduated at the top of his class but wanted to give off the image of a thug by throwing around his New York swag. He tended to pair his Timberland boots and saggy jeans with Ebonics or broken English. It was like he was fresh out of the movie *Juice*. Specifically, Tupac's character Bishop.

"So, you're going to avoid my question Dominique?"

"I thought we were ha—"

"Your dish is hot so be careful," Desha said as she looked from me to Wyatt. Her smile screamed naughtiness. "I'm sorry, D didn't say she had a date joining her. May I get something started for you, sir?"

"Sure ma'am. Let me get the Whole Shebang. I'm a little hungry and I'm not sure if I want fish, shrimp, oyster, or what, so let me get it all," he smiled. For the first time since I'd known him, I noticed his perfect teeth. There went the quiver in my thighs again. *Jesus, what am I doing with this man? He's white, why is he turning my pro-black ass on? I mean since I'm pro-black, does that mean I have to be anti-white?*

"Dommie? Dommie? Helloooooo?" Wyatt waved his hand in front of me. I was embarrassed because I felt myself biting my lip seductively.

When I looked at Desha, she had a smile on her face that told it all. "Did you want me to bring you another strawberry-lemonade? Also, do you want me to put your plate in the warmer until your date's food is ready?" she asked.

"He's not my date, we just ran into each other here. We work together. Dassit, dasall." When that rolled off my lips, I took notice of Wyatt's look of defeat. I mean, he said he didn't want any smoke between he and Spence so, why was he looking defeated.

"If you say so, love. But is that a yes or no and to one or both questions," she asked placing all of her weight on one side.

"Yes to both Desha, thanks." She was throwing good shade.

"Sir, can I get you a drink?"

"Yes ma'am. I think I'll need something a little stronger than lemonade."

"Dark or clear?" She queried.

"Dark," he smiled.

Was it really that simple to find out what kind of drink he wanted? I made it into a science project the night he came over, I thought.

Desha scurried off to get our drinks and she came back with a double shot of whatever. Wyatt sipped and nodded in agreement of her choice. I wanted to know what it was but I didn't want to seem like I was being petty by asking. Had she known what to get because the restaurant was frequented by white men? *Did I not know because I was low-key ethnocentric?*

We held friendly conversation until our food arrived. We found out a lot about each other. There was so much we had in common. Other than me being an only child and him being the oldest of two, we were basically the same person.

Once we finished our lunch, I realized that the alone time was well needed. I thanked him for being transparent with me and we headed to the exit. I was so engrossed in what he was saying, I hadn't taken notice of my surroundings.

"Bitch, can you watch where the fu–" Latrice's rant was cut short when she noticed it was me.

"You were saying?" I questioned with a raised eyebrow while cracking my knuckles. "This has been brewing for years, bitch," I growled.

Before I could grab that braided ponytail, that shit-talking bitch took off and I was hot on her trail. She had me by several steps, ole scary-ass hoe. Hopping into her car, she'd already started it up and was letting the windows all the way up.

Due to it being warm outside, we left our windows cracked to keep the heat from encasing the cars as quickly when they were unoccupied. Anyhow, I circled the car banging on the hood and the windows. "C'mon bestie, get out please. I just want to talk to you, we need closure," I said.

She placed a small crack in the window to have our conversation. "Nah, you stupid bitch. You mad 'bout that lil' fifteen hunnit a bitch took like you needed it with yo' rich spoiled ass," she yelled through the window. "I'm not getting out. You better leave me alone before I call them folks," she whined.

"Really, best friend? You gone do that to me after all these years," I probed.

"Try me hoe," she held up her phone, showing that the nine had already been touched. "Better yet bitch, if you don't get away from my car, I will call Spence and tell him that you down here caking with the white boy," she grinned devilishly.

That pissed me off so bad, I started kicking her car door. "The fuck you mean you gone call Spence? Y'all fuckin' now?" I kicked the car harder and she screamed.

"Wouldn't you like to know, hoe?" she stuck her tongue out like Cardi B does in her videos. "Bitch you don't want it. You know good and well I will stomp your ass! Kick my fuckin' Benz one more time," she mustered up a little courage inside of her safe place.

I kicked the car with the strength of every angry, abused black woman in the world. The car shook, and I left my mark. There was a huge indentation when I took my foot down.

"Dommie, that's enough. You know that girl can't fight. Leave her alone before all these nosey-ass white folks call the cops. I will not stand by and let you become the focus of a Black Lives Matter campaign for a whore. She ain't worth it," Wyatt took a breath. "Baby, let's go."

Did he call me baby? I thought. Nonetheless, what he said made sense. However, I had one more thing to get off my chest. "I know where you live, hoe. I'll be waiting in your driveway," I spat on her window. It was enough for a little to seep through the crack landing on her face. With that, Latrice peeled out on two wheels. All that was left of her was screeching tires and a cloud of smoke.

"Dommie, you know if I gotta keep you with me, you won't be in that scary ass girl's driveway," Wyatt called to me. I was breathing fire.

"No worries love, that hoe won't be in her driveway either. She know these hands is lethal. She would sleep at her mom's before she went home to this ass-whooping and she loathes her mother." We laughed at Latrice's expense, shared a hug, and promised to catch up to one another later.

I jumped into my Audi and headed out. I wouldn't allow Tricey's whorish ass to disturb my peace. Once I made it to my house, I noticed Spence's Tundra. "Fuck my life, what the hell does he want?" I spoke to myself as I cut the engine. I got out and headed into my apartment.

"Where the fuck you been?" he questioned with a scowl on his face.

And the bullshit begins...

Chapter Ten
"She's Always A Woman To Me"
Wyatt

I t's been a hot minute that I'd heard anything from Dominique. She hadn't responded to any of my text messages since the day we left Parrain's. Her disappearing act was unnerving, to say the least. Speaking of missing in action, I hadn't seen Latrice around the club and had been told if I was to see her, not to let her in. I guess her days of fucking people's men and giving them the clap was over. A few of my guys had come down from New York. We were gonna hit Club Raggs tomorrow, but then I wanted to see *her* today.

I didn't want the fellas to see her in that light but fuck it, it was a job. A great paying job at that. "Yo, y'all wanna go to the strip club, son?" I asked them as we sat around. Some of us were playing dominoes, while others were chillin' watching television. However, we all had drinks in our hands.

"Hell yeah, nigga. Take us to your club too, son," my dude Nasir slurred. His ass was always the first one to get twisted. He'd been smoking that good grass that he smuggled through security from back home, on top of drinking. I wondered how, but in the same breath, the less I knew, the better.

"It's not my club, yo. It's the club I work at," I clarified.

"Yeah, whatever son. Just take us, yo," he looked at me in disbelief. I didn't understand why my boy thought that it was my club. Actually they all thought that, I had to make sure I introduced them to C-Note, so they could get that out of their heads.

We all showered and got dressed. Although I lived in south Baton Rouge, I also owned an estate that housed five bedrooms, six baths, and a pool. It was five-thousand six-hundred fifty-eight square feet. When Dommie asked me what I was doing on that side of town, I was honestly just coming from my home. My house in the south was where I had my studio.

For those of you familiar with the Big Raggedy, you probably thinking really? The south? To answer that, yeah! Isn't it where all the talent is? Most artists I dealt with lived around the studio. Plus, I had top of the line security measures so, there was no breaking in and getting away with my state-of-the-art equipment. Aside from that, I had three grown ass pit bulls that would kill anything that crossed the threshold when I wasn't there. Those were my secret security guards, no one had ever seen them.

None of that is neither here nor there. We all piled up in my G-Wagon and headed to Purple Haze. Clowning all the way there, we pulled into the parking spot that read *Head of Security*, and everybody busted up laughing.

"The fuck y'all laughing at?" I quizzed. Confused as hell.

"Nigga, someone parked that old ass, vintage ass Cadillac in ya shit and you gotta park in the security guard spot," Raheem laughed.

"Boy if you don't shut ya ugly ass up, bro. I told y'all this ain't my spot, I am head of security." They looked at me crazy.

"With all the loot you got, you really working for another nigga?" Abdul asked

"Bro, I keep telling you, wealth is quiet and reserved. Rich is loud and messy. I don't need muthafuckas all in my pockets when it comes to studio time. Assuming they can run out on me because I got it. Are you gonna visit me in Louisiana State Penitentiary?" Everyone got quiet. "I didn't think so."

Walking up to the door as a normal patron, Fred looked at me and was taken aback.

"What it's hittin' fa, my nigga?" he dapped me up. "I didn't recognize you, all labeled up and shit, ya feel me," he referred to my Balmain outfit paired with Bally Hakem ST- High top sneakers. Oh yeah, a brother was fly.

"Ain't nothing bro, me and my New York fam came in to see what's good. You know I never get to see the club from the customer's point of view," I grinned cheekily. "I'm tryna see these asses clap tonight."

As we passed through the longest line I'd seen in a few weeks, I heard my favorite dancer's theme song drop.

> Those innocent eyes(eyes), That smile on your face makes it easy to trust you, If they only knew, the girl with the tattoo, like I do. Doin' what you doin' just to get you where you goin', yeah I see, baby.

We cut through the hallway and into the showroom. There she was on stage, giving the sexiest performance of all the dancers in the building. Mind you, Dominique may not have been the baddest female in the building to everyone else, however she was the only one I was checking for.

Each time that I had been in her presence, I was more captivated by her beauty. And because I'm not a shallow guy, I don't mean what her outside looked like. Her personality and her heart were getting to my heart. I hated the mere fact that she was my ex-homie's girl. In my mind, it didn't matter whose girl she was, I wanted her, and I was going to have her.

Initially, I didn't want to pursue her because of Spence, but if I'm honest, he doesn't deserve her. A good woman doesn't scratch the surface of a description of Dominique. She's smart, caring, funny, witty, charming and she's damn sure sexy.

The sight before me was mesmerizing. Dominique was in her *Unique* zone, doing her shit, owning the stage like a champ. She cat crawled to the pole, flipped, climbed the pole and slid down in a split. The crowd went wild and so did my woody.

"Yo, who the fuck is that, my nigga? She a bad bitch dude," Nasir yelled over the loud music.

My blood boiled a lil' bit and she wasn't mine... yet! "Yo, you don't see her name lit up behind her? That's Unique, one of the main money-makers in here."

"Don't state the obvious," he laughed and headed toward the stage to make it rain on her.

I headed to the bar and had a seat. Arronisha hooked me up with a double shot of Evan Williams. We shot the shit for a lil' while and I learned a little about her other than her cool, calm, and collected demeanor.

"Unique up there killing the stage tonight, huh boo?" she asked.

"To be honest, this is my first time ever really watching her perform. She has so much elegance and self-confidence. It's more like she's ballet dancing instead of stripping," I stared at the stage as she finished her three-song set.

"I see you salivating boo," Arronisha laughed.

"Nah, she got a man on her team. I don't do well on the sidelines, feel me?" I retorted.

Dommie got off stage and made her rounds. She gave a few lap dances and I took notice of something I hadn't noticed earlier. Her face was caked with make-up and she was searching the room for someone.

Looking around the club, I took notice of Spence's fuck ass. He wasn't looking at me nor Dominique, he looked at another stripper with lust-filled eyes like she was his woman. He never once paid attention to the safety or well-being of his girl. That shit was fucked up. All at her job being a buster.

After another drink, I decided to head over to C-Note's office, so he could come out and meet my family. These fools gone be laughing their asses off when they meet him. He's five-foot-two, small-framed, and not too appealing to the eye. These women love him though. Once they start working here, they don't wanna go to any other club.

After all was said and done, we headed to the car discussing what to eat, IHOP or Waffle House.

"Who was the girl with the tattooed thighs?" Abdul asked.

He was the second of the crew to check for Dominique.

"That's my bitch, nigga," I heard Spencer say behind us.

"Yooooo, I know this ain't who the fuck I think it is talking shit behind me," Abdul exclaimed. I saw the happiness in his eyes to hear Spence's voice.

Nasir and Raheem turned to face Spence. "What's up my guy," they blurted in unison.

"Don't tell me y'all two niggas still on that fuck shit about what happened with Aileen." Nasir slurred, noticing the tension between us. "That shit happened when we were in high school. Let that shit go, yo," he finished.

Paying none of them fools any mind, I went to stand near my truck. Spence's eyes lit up like a kid's at Christmas when he'd walked in and saw his new bike for the first time. I stood there thinking about a lot of things. Maybe they were right, maybe I should let that shit go. I mean, it was almost eight years ago. Yeah, I can let that go. I don't think me feeling his girl will mull over too well, however.

As the fellas dapped him up and headed towards the truck, I decided to squash the beef that had been ongoing for too many years. Surprisingly, he was headed in my direction as I was his.

"Yo, let me holla at you, Spence," I requested.

"What's good, son? I was on my way to say a few words to you too, my nigga," he replied.

"I just wanna let you know that life is too short to beef over something as trivial as what we are beefing over, son. My sister gave it up to you, I know. However, at the time all I could think of was you, my brother had betrayed me," I thought back.

"Well, look. What I have to say to you may not sit well," he paused. "I really appreciate you wanting to squash that shit my nigga, but the truth is, all I give a fuck about is you staying away from Dominique. She's my girl and I know you only trying to get at her to get back at me," I looked at him crazily.

"Nigga, what?" I quizzed. I only use nigga amongst my homeboys because it was what we M.I.S.F.I.T.S. called each other. It wasn't until later in life that I found out it was a derogatory term used to degrade blacks. "Stay away from Dominique? She's my homegirl and I protect her from drunk fools in the club. You can't be serious, yo," I gritted.

"Nigga, I watched you salivate over my bitch while you sat at the bar lusting and laughing with old girl. I bet that red-head, drink-serving bitch tried to encourage you to slide in," he growled.

I stepped to him and hemmed him up by the collar of his cheap ass shirt. At this point, Abdul had grabbed hold of Spence and Nas and Ra had grabbed me. "Cut the shit yo, let 'em go bro," Ra begged.

"Yo, listen man. Arronisha is good people and you won't disrespect her like that. She only sees the good in everyone, and even though she knows you're a snake, all she does is pray that Dominique cuts her grass soon," I shoved him away from me.

"You's a fuckboy, Snow. You always have been. Stay away from my bitch or else!" Spence threatened.

"Or what? You gone beat my ass like you did last time?" I laughed in his bitch-made face simply because I had dusted his bitch ass a few years ago. "Or are you gone beat my ass like you do Dominique to keep her in line?" No sooner than the words fell from my mouth, I heard a familiar voice.

"You ready to go, baby?" Dominique cooed. She walked up from behind me hugging Spencer.

"This is my bitch, nigga. Do yourself a favor and stay away from her," he threatened and kissed her cheek.

"Man, let's go, yo," I said to the fellas.

We piled into my truck and headed into the direction of IHOP. I didn't care where we went at that point, I had allowed Spencer to get under my skin. The way Dommie looked at me when he kissed her let me know that she'd heard me arguing with him. I felt like shit.

Hopping out of the truck, I noticed Halo's SS Impala. I knew it was hers because she was the only person in the city with that particular blue candy-paint job. We walked in and it hadn't gotten too crowded yet, therefore, we were seated within moments.

After ordering food, our drinks came. We sat and they clowned with one another for a few minutes trying to ease the tension. They knew when I was pissed, I didn't wanna talk or laugh, so I initiated small talk. I laughed a little with the fellas and headed to the restroom. Turning the corner for the restrooms, I bumped into Dominique.

"I thought you left with Spencer?" I stated confused.

"Don't talk to me," she looked at me with every morsel of hurt and anguish in her eyes. "I never told you that he put his hands on me, but there you stood, using it against him," she pointed out.

"I never meant to hurt you in the process of gut punching him. I promise, it was a low blow, and I apologize for making it look like you pillow talk with me," I pleaded.

"Save that bullshit, Wyatt," she gritted and headed towards her table.

My heart was broken. I couldn't believe I had stooped that low in effort to put Spencer on front street as an abuser, but hurt a queen in the course of our argument. In that moment, I knew that I didn't deserve another moment of her time nor her friendship. I should have talked to her about the abuse that I had taken a mental note of, not used it as a weapon in a battle between myself and my childhood friend turned rival.

Chapter Eleven
"My Pride Is All I Have"
Dominique

I couldn't believe what I'd heard about Wyatt. Here I was thinking he could be that guy, the one I'd find my soul mate in. I guess men were men, it didn't matter what color they were. White men weren't any different from black men. They were all self-centered assholes that fought for a prize, and beat their chests when they won. Tuh, the fuck they thought, I was no one's goddamn property.

Pulling into my parking spot after having the routine lunch date with my parents, I was relieved to see that Spencer's ugly community dick ass wasn't at my crib. He had been distant since I'd beat his ass and that was fine with me. The shit he pulled last weekend at the club was frivolous. He knew good and well that I didn't get down with him like that, but because I played along with his performance to get back at Wyatt, he thought everything was kosher.

I pulled up to my usual parking spot and got out. After rounding the corner and cutting under the stairwell, I noticed Felicity walking away from my door.

"Hey love, what's good?" I called out excitedly.

"Hey boo, I was just stopping by to see if you were up for company for a few minutes," she smiled.

"Sure, c'mon in. I have lunch with my parents every Sunday afternoon, like clockwork," I informed her. We had been hanging out with each other since the icebreaker that took place at Winn-Dixie that day. She was a pretty dope chick. I was blown away by her history. It included everything but love. Sadly, I knew she harbored a lot of hatred as an adolescent. Here I thought she was a bitch just because. Getting to know her taught me the true meaning of not judging a book by its cover.

"Girl, yo shit laid. I knew you prolly had some nice shit, but I didn't think it would be Pier 1 Imports nice," she praised the furniture in my apartment..

"Child, these are merely things. My mother got most of it for me," I shrugged. "What's up, Hun?" I quizzed. As many a times as we'd hung out, she had never been to my crib. I was almost certain that she had something on her mind.

"I just wanted to hang out. I have a lot of hoes around me, but no friends. Not for real," she admitted. It was sad to hear her say that, but I knew exactly how she felt.

All my life I had my best friend Victoria, Tricey, and Tricey's younger sister Lestlee in my corner, I was fine with them until I no longer was. Once we graduated high school, Tori moved to England to study abroad at University of Arts London.

When she came back to the States, she made her life in Los Angeles and worked for Paramount Pictures doing on-set wardrobe changes for actresses.

Nonetheless, the more females, the more drama, and I despised drama. Despising it never kept me out of it, unfortunately. Merely being friends with Lestlee and her messy ass sister, kept me in something that ended up in me kicking ass, and them watching the match. Although, Lee was younger, she'd attempt to help but would be held back by Latrice's scary ass.

Even with all of that in the shadows, I didn't catch onto Tricey wanting me to fail. I always thought she loved me. Even if Tricey was up to no good, I assumed Lestlee and I were sisters forever. Our own parents couldn't tell us any different, that's how tight we were.

"Girl, do you hear me talking to you?" Felicity interrupted my thoughts.

"Sorry boo, I had zoned out like a mofo." We laughed.

"You wanna talk about it?" she responded.

"Nah, it's old news. Nothing to really dwell on, my girl."

"Rumor has it that you're the golden gloves champion of your high school," she said.

"Now who would start that lie?" I laughed.

"My lil' cousin Joann went to Istrouma, she said you had a few fights there because people assumed you were stuck-up and prissy. She also said that you fought mostly defending that bitch of a friend for fucking somebody boyfriend," she turned her nose up.

"Joann... Joann... Joann Jackson?" I pondered then my eyes lit up.

"Yes, she was quiet, had a sister and a brother," she shook her head in an up and down motion.

"She was a cool chick. I liked her because she stayed in her lane. She talking about me, I remember her and her sister had a fight with this chick and her boyfriend's sister jumped in. I was at my aunt's house when it happened. That shit was crazy. Then this girl that lived across the street came out of nowhere and clocked the girl she was fighting," I laughed until tears welled in my eyes. That was some crazy shit to watch.

"The girl in the white house with green trim that sat on the corner?" Felicity asked.

"Yeah. She was drilling that poor little girl."

"That was me, bitch!" We both busted up laughing. It was like we were inside of the laugh factory. "Ok, ok, ok. Let's breathe for a minute." We laughed more and caught our breaths. "I won a pair of front row tickets to the On The Run tour, would you like to go with me?" she looked at me.

"Stop lying, chick. I been trying to find tickets for months. That shit was sold out since the day tickets went on sale," I was taken aback by the fact that she had won a pair.

"I ain't lying, I'm dead ass serious. I'm literally on my way to the studio to pick up the tickets and to the Mall of Louisiana to see if I can find something cute to wear," she informed me.

"Am I an afterthought, bitch?" I questioned.

"No, crazy ass girl. I just said I didn't have the tickets yet. Do you want the extra ticket or not?"

"I mean, even if I was, I'd still be sitting right next to that ass next Saturday. I love the Carters. Did you want me to roll with you? I gotta find a fit, too. It's only two-thirty, we should go to the city, so we can hit Canal Place."

"Yes lawd, now you are speaking my language. Saks and Solstice, here I come," she sang out.

Grabbing my purse and keys to lock up, she agreed to drive. We walked two buildings over to her apartment to grab her wallet and headed out.

$$$$

"Girl, so you know White Chocolate is digging you, right?" she rumored.

"Here you go with them shits, that man does not like me like that. We were friends until that night I overheard him talking shit to Spence."

"The way he was looking at you in IHOP says he wanna get up in them thighs," she laughed. "I'on know sus, I think he tryna make an ice cream sandwich."

"You and your damn analogies get on my damn nerves," I laughed. She looked at me for a moment then joined in on the laughter.

We turned into our gated driveway and she put her keycode into the box. I had a great day today and was excited to be going to see Jay-Z and Beyoncé. That particular couple reminds me of the dream Spencer sold me about becoming a power couple.

Pulling into the open parking spot next to my car, I noticed several lights on throughout my apartment. I was flipping out because I knew I had turned all of the lights off except the one over the stove prior to leaving. "What the fuck?" I questioned just above a whisper.

"What's going on, suge?" Felicity raised her perfectly arched brow.

"I may be tripping but it looks like a lot of lights are on in my apartment. I'm not going to freak out because your headlights are shining through the window and it may be the reflection bouncing off the glass."

Pulling her gun from a concealed area underneath the steering wheel, she cocked it and smiled. "Let's go check that shit out," she hopped out like she was Cagney and I was Lacey.

Some people had no idea who Cagney and Lacey were when I'd mention them back in the day. They were a pair of female police officers that were on a squad in a New York based television program. My nanny was a huge fan of them, therefore, I also watched the show and became a huge fan.

"Hold up," I called out to her as I popped the locks on my Audi and grabbed the .38 special from its holster.

As I readied myself for the best, but prepared myself for the worst. I placed my key in the keyhole and entered my apartment. The sight before me was normal. My place wasn't ransacked, leaving everything in its rightful place. I ran straight to my room with Felicity stopping of to check the second bedroom and the hallway bathroom.

Walking into my room with guns drawn, I noticed the closet door and all of Spencer's drawers hanging open. Immediately, I knew it was him that had come into my apartment. With no intent other than to spite me, he did what he knew would drive me up the wall. He turned every freaking light on in the house. "That son of a biiiiitch!" I yelled at the top of my lungs!

"What happened?" Felicity startled me.

"That dirty motherfucker came in, took all his shit, and left," I declared as I walked toward the closet. "NO! No, no, no. He didn't do this shit to me!" I cried.

"What?" Felicity said with as much angst in her tone as I had.

"He took every dime from my safe and the jewelry from my jewelry box," I yelped and fell to my knees. "He could've taken every piece of jewelry he wanted but those pieces were family heirlooms. I'm gonna fucking kill him!"

"Check this shit out, ma," she handed me a folded note with my name on it.

Opening the neatly folded letter, my heart pounded out of my chest. I took a deep breath and started to read it.

> Look, I ain't with this relationship no mo. I took all my shit and some of yours since you can afford to replace it. You're a self-centered bitch and I'm leaving you for your best friend. She's pregnant with my kid and she's the bitch that gave you gonorrhea. Thanks for all the years of not knowing how to be the woman I needed. Fuck you have a nice life.
>
> P.S. I know that charm meant a lot to you, but it looks better on Sharae. She will wear it on our wedding day.
>
> -Spence

It was a low blow. It felt like I had been gut-punched and all the wind had been sucked from my lungs. I couldn't breathe. I just wanted to wake up and the nightmare be over. This shit wasn't happening to me. I'd been hurt by two people that I had never given a reason to hate me so bad to fuck over me in such a way.

"True I was done with him friend, but her? He left me for her, though?" I asked rhetorically.

"Friend, I know we been tough, and you know that I'm cut from a different cloth so when I say what I have to say, don't set trip." Felicity looked at me.

"Well this sounds like the start of a fucked-up conversation. But I feel like I need to hear what you gotta say. Go ahead and tell me whatever it is you gotta tell me, hell," I looked at her with misty eyes.

"I know what they did to you was fucked up. The truth is, everyone knew they been fucking except you. I never took you for a weak bitch, but you can't be blind. I always thought you knew but were ok with it. When we started hanging out, I wanted to ask you, but I didn't want to dabble into anyone's business. Your sexual life, to me, was off limits. Know what I'm saying?" She looked at me as if I was insane.

"I knew he was cheating, but not with her. I can't believe I've been naïve to him fucking my ex-best friend. I guess that's prolly why she threatened to call him two weeks ago when I was about to get in that ass... funny thing is, he's leaving me because she supposedly pregnant," I fell into a fit of laughter.

"Bitch, you good though?" Felicity asked as she inched her way to the room door.

"Yeah, I'm great. The fuckin jokes on him because that hoe can't have babies. I'mma roll with it, because it's not my story to tell. I guess his slow ass will figure out she lied when she never starts to show," I mumbled. Even though they'd done the illest shit they could do to me, I still couldn't find humor in her disability to bear a child.

"What?" she laughed, and I cut my eyes at her. "Hey, that bitch did you dirty. Don't tell me you feel some type of way because I laughed," she scolded me.

"You know, it is pretty humorous. Not because she can't have kids, but because... she can't have kids!" I yelled in a fit of laughter. I was holding my stomach I laughed so hard. "She fooled his duck ass to think she was pregnant. I gotta admit, they played me. I allowed it to happen so I'm good on that issue."

"I know I just said your sex life was off limits, but I gotta know this particular detail," Felicity implied.

"Oh lawd chile, what is it?"

"No lies, bitch. When was the last time y'all had sex?" she questioned. Her beautiful face was etched with worry overpowered by seriousness.

"I'm almost scared to answer that, love," I replied as sweat beads started to build on my philtrum.

"Just answer the question," she softened as she walked over to me and pulled me down to sit next to her at the foot of my bed.

"Two and a half maybe three months ago," I admitted. "He gave me gonorrhea and I said then that I wasn't fucking him anymore."

"Maybe you dodged the bullet, girl," she responded.

I was a bit confused because I had just admitted to a sexually transmitted disease. She said I may have dodged a bullet, however I felt like I got shot dead between the eyes. I was almost certain that this conversation would be much worse than I could ever imagine.

"Beating around the bush has never helped the bush grow. Just tell me what you got to say, Felicity," I grilled.

She blew out a healthy breath, giving me a look of consternation. I felt bile building up in my throat, I was so nervous for what I was preparing myself to hear.

A tear rolled from her eye and she spoke. "I wish I hadn't been so judgmental of you before I got to know you," she started. "I knew the bitch was burning niggas, she had been doing that for a while before you started dancing. I regret to tell you this, but you need to know," she cried, causing me to squeeze her hand as if she was the one that needed consoling.

"It can't be that bad, right?" I cautioned.

"Friend, I'mma give it to you straight no chaser because I respect you," she swiped the tears from her eyes. "I need you to set an appointment to have a full sexually transmitted disease panel run on you. Alizé got fired from the club a few weeks ago. Word on the street is that she was let go because someone at the Health Unit leaked her results. Supposedly, she's HIV positive," she sniffed. It was now her turn to squeeze my hand reassuringly.

My heart skipped several beats following her revelation. I was stuck in a time warp. The words that had left her lips were looping like a song on repeat. *HIV positive. HIV positive. HIV positive.* I didn't know if she'd said anything following those two words and if she had, I didn't hear her.

"Friend," I heard in the distance although she sat inches away from me. "Friend, talk to me," she said. "Dominique, if you don't answer me I'mma be forced to smack you."

"Bitch, if you smack me we gonna be fighting up in here. That's on God," I finally responded.

I was breathing fire as well as sick to the pit of my stomach. I was blind-sided by two dirty motherfuckers and they are gonna pay what the fuck they owe.

"It's time to pay the fucking piper. I have taken a lot of punches from these hoes. The meek version of me is no longer available. It's time to release the beast."

"I'm down for whatever, let's go to that hoe house and beat her monkey-ass," Felicity chimed in.

"Nah, fuck that. I'mma kill both of 'em," I said seriously.

"Ha, ha, ha, ha. Bitch you crazy as fuck," she laughed causing me to give her a death stare. "Oh, you serious?" she said after seizing her fit of laughter.

"Fucking well right I'm serious," I replied. "So you down or not?"

"Friend, I don't think murder should be in the cards when they already dying. Let them hoes love each other and die slowly. Fuck them bitches, they deserve each other. Nasty asses," she explained. "Now if you wanna fight a bitch, flatten some tires, put a lil' sugar in the tank, maybe even burn a bitch's house down... I'm that bitch," she made sense but not fucking really.

"All of the above, let's get it," I went into the living room and felt like I was suffering from a detrimental dysfunction. I'mma do everything in my power to make them feel the wrath of a scorned good woman and great friend.

After grabbing my keys and wallet we headed out. Felicity hopped into her car and cranked it up. I hopped into the passenger seat and she switched the music to some *fuck it up* type shit.

Hey! Got some static for some niggas on the other side of town, Let my little cousin K roll, he's a rider now, What they want from us motherfuckin' thug niggas? Used to love niggas now I plug niggas, and slug niggas, Am I wrong? Niggas makin' songs, tryin' to get with us...

The late Tupac's sexy ass voice boomed through the sound system. We bobbed our heads, she put her car into reverse, and began to back out. The car started rolling back and we were cut off by an oversized G-Wagon. I had seen it somewhere before, but a bitch didn't have time to see who was in it. I was on a mission.

Honk, honk, hoooooonk!

"Get the fuuuuuck outta the waaaaay!" Felicity yelled over the music.

Whoever it was, hopped out of their truck as we both jumped out of her ride with pistols in our hand. We were ready to take it to the streets, down for whatever.

"Whoa, slow down killers. What y'all got going on?" the driver asked.

"Why are you here, Wyatt?" I grilled.

"Come ride with me. What's good, Felicity?" he responded.

"Nah, I'm busy. I'm 'bout to go get dicked down and beat on by that nigga. Go on and get in ya truck so I can handle that, ya feel me," I said and headed back to the door to get in.

"Dominique stop walking, dammit," he demanded. "Get in my truck so we can go for a ride. I need to talk to you."

"Nah white boy, you good!" I said before sitting and closing the door.

"Can you move so I can back out?" Felicity chimed in.

"Felicity, can I speak to you?" he quizzed.

Mr. Charming pulled his card and won Felicity over. They stood near his truck as she listened intently with a few nods of her head. After moments of watching them interact and converse back and forth, I decided to get out of the car. I knew she wasn't into Wyatt nor was he into her, however I needed to find out what was so secretive. The way she kept looking back at me made me uncomfortable.

"The fuck y'all talking about?" I queried upon approach.

"Oh, we were definitely talking about you!" Wyatt said.

Felicity smiled like a Cheshire Cat, which made me uneasy. It was like he'd let her in on a secret and I felt some type of way. I wanted to know what was so funny when we were just headed to beat two bitches down. "What's up, Snow?" I asked as I approached them.

"Snow?" Felicity asked confused.

"Yeah, that's my nickname. Me and my crew from back in the day were all misfits. That was the name they gave me because I was the white dude of the crew," he laughed just like he did when he explained.

"Yeah, yeah. We were headed out, so what's good?" I asked again.

"Yo, slow ya roll lil' mama. I don't know who pissed in your cereal, but I do know it wasn't me. I came over to talk to you I need you to hear me out." The look in his eyes reached my thighs.

I knew that if I had left with him, he was gonna be satisfying my cookie's craving for him. But judging by the twinkle in Felicity's eyes, she was no longer interested in helping me get revenge on Spencer and Sharae's dirty asses.

"Look Snow, I don't know what you want from me. Whatever you're trying to sell, I'm not buying."

"Dominique, I'm jus—"

"Wyatt, give us a minute please," Felicity butted in cutting him off. Grabbing me by the arm she led me to the sidewalk in front of her still running car. "What is your problem, friend?" she asked. "This man is trying."

"Trying what? To fuck? I ain't into him like that."

"Why not bitch? Cuz he's white?" She shot back.

"No, because I heard him talking shit to Spencer about me like I was a piece of meat."

"Bitch, when? What I remember was him talking shit to Spencer about how small of a man he was for putting his hands on you. From what you told me out of your own mouth was that he taunted him, trying to get Spencer to step to him like he stepped to you. Correct me if I'm wrong, friend."

"You're right, love. I'm just not ready to move on..." I stated somberly.

"Who said you had to move on? This man just wants to talk to you. Hear him out friend, damn," she hugged me like a sister, walked over to her car, and closed the passenger door.

By then Wyatt had already moved his truck into an empty parking space. Backing out, Felicity rolled the passenger's side window down. I looked to her to save me, instead she hit me with something less than ignorant. "Don't get pregnant with the white man's baby," she yelled, then skidded out towards her building.

Looking to the left of me, I noticed Wyatt laughing.

"What's so funny? Ain't no reason for you to laugh," I questioned with an attitude. I approached his truck and hopped in the passenger side. I put on my seatbelt, folded my arms, and pouted like a brat.

"Let's dip, Dommie," he laughed some more.

Chapter Twelve
"Her Heart Won't Let Me Lose Her"
Wyatt

I t was like pulling chicken teeth to get Dominique to take a ride with me. Had it not been for Felicity, I may have not gotten her to hear me out. Even after getting her in my truck, we still had to stop near Felicity's crib to get Dominique's shopping bags. She acted as if she wouldn't see Felicity nor her bags before attending the On The Run Tour with Jay-Z and the Bey. I wasn't much a fan of the duo, but I did dig everything they did solo.

"What do you want, Snow?" Dominque called out, breaking the silence in the cab of my truck.

"You," I said simply.

I felt heat on the side of my face as we pulled up to the intersection at Highland Road and Airline Highway. I came to a stop due to the traffic light turning red. I caught her glaring at me.

"You asked. I told you that I would always be honest with you. There you have it, love," I stated in a smooth tone.

After a few more minutes, we took a left into the gated entrance of the community that I lived in. The look on Dominique's face gave a wave of discomfort. It was more of a nervous rather than shocked expression. The security guard walked up to the truck and greeted both her and me by name.

"Mr. O'Sullivan, Ms. Johnson, have a great evening," the gate keeper said.

"Thanks Jimmy," we said in unison.

"How do you know the security guard?" I quizzed.

"My parents' house is here. I was raised here and went to school on the other side of town because I didn't want to be the oddball out."

"What do you mean the oddball out?" I asked.

"C'mon Snow. You know what your neighbors look like. Me in school with their kids, I'd be the darkest one in class. No diversity at all," she admitted.

"Both my neighbors look like you. However, I follow. It's the same reason I caught the ferry to Queens most of the week. The only difference was, our outer appearances were the same. I felt like I stuck out like a sore thumb in our community because I was different on the inside."

Pulling into my driveway, Dommie stared at my neighbor's house. It was like she was in awe. Her admiration of the home had me feeling slighted. Here we were in the driveway of my huge ass house and she stared at theirs. Their shit was tighter than mine, but damn. What a way to make me feel bad.

"You and my parents are neighbors? Small freaking world," she put her hand over her face.

"No way, Ron and Cassie are your parents?" I asked. "You're right it's a small world. Those are my folks. Ron has been trying to introduce us for months now. Low and behold, we already know each other," I laughed.

"So you're the handsome young neighbor that mother has talked about all this time. Every time I come over I beg her and daddy not to go over to get you," she laughed. "She never once mentioned that the neighbor was white," she said just above a whisper.

"Maybe because my outer appearance only matters to you," I replied which warranted her evil glare, once again.

Cutting the engine, we got out and walked inside of my home. Her shock gauge was off the chart, I saw the surprise in her eyes. I waited for her to ask when I'd moved here since everyone assumed I lived in south Baton Rouge. She wasn't one of those girls, because she never asked.

"What do you want, Wyatt?" she asked for at least the thousandth time tonight. Of course the amount of times was exaggerated, but to me, that's how it felt.

"What I want is the chance to tell you what I should've told you when we first started talking to one another. I didn't think I would get to a point of caring about you the way I do so, I didn't find it necessary."

We stood in my foyer, staring at one another as seconds passed. Not saying a word, she looked at me as if she was searching my eyes for my heart, my mind, or even my soul. Grabbing her by the hand, I led her into the den and settled us on the couch. I wanted this woman, I cared about the hurt in her eyes and in her heart. I craved being the one to make her smile and exude happiness.

I wanted to be the one to teach her how to own her worth and get rid of past transgressions, namely Latrice and Spence's punk ass. I wasn't the guy who was into fixing people. I never believed that people could be fixed, we're human, not objects. I believed in teaching people how to love themselves to a point that nothing was longed for in order to validate them besides their own thoughts.

Don't get me wrong, validation is appreciated, however it isn't necessary. I was raised in a home where love was in abundance. My mother and father adored each other. They came from two totally different classes. One family loathed the other because of financial status. They were like the Hatfields and the McCoys, except my parents were the territory. I guess in a sense, it would've been more like the story of Noah and Allie from the book turned movie, *The Notebook*. My dad was poor, and my mother was of the elite back in Ireland.

"Say what you gotta say and take me home, please," Dommie butted into my thoughts.

"Why are you so upset? I came to your house just in time to save you from doing something you were sure to regret."

"Nah, don't try to redirect this conversation... what's good?" she responded with a no-nonsense demeanor.

"Listen, I don't want you to be mad or upset about what I'm gonna tell you. I know it's gonna look bad when I say what it is I have to say."

"I'm sure it can't be any worse than any of the other news I've heard today. Go ahead and put the cherry on top of the shit."

"I've known Spencer for the biggest part of my life. We have a very extensive history," I started.

"The fuck that mean, don't tell me y'all on some gay shit. The nigga already fucking my ex-best friend who possibly has HIV. I don't know if I would be able to let his fuck ass live knowing that he been fucking men too," she huffed as her chest heaved rapidly.

"Fuck no. Lil' mama, you trying my life right now. I don't do dick in my hand, my mouth, or my ass. Nor am I fond of my dick being in a hard man's mouth, hand, or ass. Yo, you got me fucked up, son," I ranted.

She laughed so hard at my response, I couldn't help but to join her in laughter. The tears of joyfulness that poured from her eyes made me content. I was happy to be able to bring that emotion out of her.

"Boy, if you could've seen your face you'd understand. You can carry on," she giggled.

"Anyway," I chuckled because she was still laughing. "I have known Spence since I was 9 years old. Remember when I told you I use to catch the ferry to Queens and was a part of a group called the M.I.S.F.I.T.S.?" I paused.

"Yeah," she responded.

"He was part of that group."

"Okay? What's your point?" She prompted.

"Point is, when I met you in the club, I had no idea you were Spence's girl. Then when I found out, I tried to stay away from you because I didn't want to seem like I was stepping on his toes as revenge for the dirty shit he did to me," I scoffed. "After the night I went to your crib to make sure Byron wasn't a threat, I can't lie and say I wasn't feeling you. I was already physically attracted to you but then we connected mentally. I'm not sure if you know how fucking dope you are, but you need to embrace it, ma," I recommended.

"Wait, I'm not about to let you skate past the part about revenge. Am I a fucking pawn in some sick game you two are playing?" she cut me off before I could continue.

"Babe, can you hear me out, please?" I asked.

"Babe? Oh, I'm babe nah? Tuh!" she responded with an attitude.

"We were CRU, I thought we would all be tough forever, you know? Then he fucked my little sister and had no remorse about it."

"The fuck?"

"Yeah. His response was she was fucking anyway so why not hit sense she approached him. That was some foul shit for him to do. I felt like had I done it to anyone in our circle, it would've been problematic. Not because I was a player but because when I love, I love hard, and they would've essentially been my law instead of my homeboy."

"But that makes no sense at all," she responded.

"Right, but as fellas and homies we had agreed that sisters were off limits. Instead, he fucked my sister, took her for eight grand, and dodged her afterwards so I beat his ass down like a dude I didn't know."

"You beat his ass?" she pursed her lips and stared in disbelief.

"I did, and I don't regret one moment of it. He was and still is a cocky motherfucka and needed to be put in his place. Don't get me wrong, it wasn't an easy feat. However, in the end, I prevailed and reigned winner of the battle."

"That's some fucked up shit," she replied.

"Yeah, it was. The night at the club, the guys made me think I could put it behind us. I approached Spence to tell him that I had finally forgiven him. Given the years that had passed and the light of the circumstances surrounding the whole ordeal, I was willing to leave it in the past. I mean, honestly, Aileen did invite him over under false pretenses to bed him," I admitted.

"Yeah but he still could've walked away."

"True, because Raheem did," I said solemnly. "That's neither here nor there. I say all of this to say, when I approached him to squash the beef, he hit me with I had better stay away from you. I was blown out of the water by his audacity. It was more or less like you were his property rather than his woman," I breathed. "I asked him how the hell was I supposed to stay away from you when we worked together. He was on some rah-rah shit so, I checked his ass. From there, you walked up on the end of the argument which leads us to the here and now," I looked keenly into her eyes.

"He told me you were only interested in me because of revenge but never told me the depth of it. I'm not gonna be a pawn in you guys' little game of war," she shot back.

"I would never do that to you, queen. All I have is dope love to give to a dope woman. I tried to walk away from you on a friendship level, the shit just didn't work, ma. Each time I tried to walk away all I could hear in my head was what my dad preached to me over and over," I smiled at the thought of the father-son time.

"What was it that he said to you? It seems like it made you feel great the way you're smiling," she questioned.

"He'd say: *Listen at me, Wyatt. When I met your mother I was piss poor, broke, and hungry but I knew that she was the one and I loved her. When I approached her I had merely a dream of being rich. We snuck around from the time we first kissed to the moment we found out she was pregnant with you. I knew then that I had to take what little I had to invest into my family. Love, happiness, and respect got us to where we are today. Love and respect was the easy part. When we figured out that happiness was not a destination but a way of travel, that was the moment we won! Whatever it is in life that you want to do, make sure the route to get there is happiness,*" I mocked in his Irish accent.

"That's a great way to look at things. I wish it was that easy," she responded with a slight grin on her beautiful face.

I reached up and grabbed her hair. Surprisingly she didn't pull away. She was in her natural state, so it was beautiful, shiny, and wavy. We sat in silence for moments as I played in her hair, her face was etched in worry or dismay. Either emotion, I wanted to fix it. I wanted to save her.

Grabbing her tiny hands, I held them in mine. She looked like she need a friend and a shoulder to cry on. I was ready to be that for her, ready to allow her to bare all with no inhibitions. Her eyes pooled with tears and my heart shattered in a million pieces.

"They took everything," she said. "What am I going to do now that I have nothing?" she allowed her head to fall onto my shoulder as she bawled her eyes out. In that moment, I knew she was in a weak, vulnerable state and I dare not take advantage of her.

I allowed her to free the caged bird. She was beautiful in that naked moment, I think my heart swelled ten times more than it had since the night at her apartment. She was beautiful then, but she is much more beautiful now.

"You came out with your life, those were just things, babe. Let them have it. They deserve each other. Especially with the rumors going around the club in lieu of why C let Latrice's trifling ass go," I gossiped like a female.

"I already know what the rumors are. I'm going to be screened first thing Monday morning. But I can't just let it go, they took a piece of jewelry that has huge sentimental value. They will either give me my shit back or they will pay." All of her hurt had turned into anger. That much emotion was evident on her beautiful face.

"Let's go get it so we can move on with life. Like I told you in the beginning, I don't do drama, but at the same time that's some fucked up shit," I admitted.

"Really? You would go with me to get my things back?" her eyes lit up.

"Of course I would. I won't let him hurt you anymore, boo. He has done enough."

"All I want is my necklace, they can have the rest. I mean, they took every dime I had worked for and saved up, but I can have that back in no time." She was so happy, she hugged my neck.

Bzzzz. Bzzzz. Her phone alerted her of a text message. Pulling the phone from her purse she looked at it in shock. I wanted to ask about it, but it wasn't my place. My curiosity was cured before long, however.

"Look at this shit," Dommie exclaimed, passing me the phone.

Tricey: Mission accomplished bitch, I finally won...

Message received 11:46 p.m.

There was a video and two photo attachments attached to the message. As I thumbed through, I acknowledged that they were all captioned and taunting Dominique for a reaction. The photos included one of Tricey standing in front of Spencer's house in Sherwood Forest captioned, "Yo nigga bought me a house". The second one was a picture of her squatting in front of a Benz that I'd seen him in on several occasions, holding a cross in her hands. The caption on that one read "Before you CROSS me," with a few crying laughing faces.

I didn't understand the depth of that one until I thought it out. That jump-off was posing in front of her ex-best friend's man's car, holding the heirloom that they'd stolen from her. I assumed that was the lowest she could get, until I watched the video.

This trick ass slut was deep throating what I assumed to be Spencer's dick. She sucked his shit up like it was melting ice cream, making it disappear like her throat was magic. Prior to the video ending, she plopped his ejaculating tool out of her mouth, smiled into the camera, then said "Real bitches swallow, we don't spit." Kissing the cum-filled tip, she proceeded to slurping up the sperm that had pooled around the grip of her hand, followed by showing her tongue to the camera, ending the show.

"Can you believe this shit?" she asked in disbelief.

"I'm biased. I think you want that answer from someone else."

"He bought her a house after all the years we've been together? The fuck kind of shit is that?" she asked.

"He didn't' buy her a house. Please tell me you've been to that house before," I prompted her for any recollection of the house in the photo.

"Not once have I ever seen that house until now. Have you been there?" she quizzed.

"Really Dommie? You know good and well I don't fuck with Spence like that. He posted pictures of him in the realtor's office closing on his Instagram and did a live walkthrough on Facebook after he got his keys. You know how people are, we brag different. The loudest ones either never had shit or ain't used to having shit," I admitted.

"Can't he just be proud of his accomplishment? And when the hell did he get social media? He hasn't had social media since I've known him," Dominique quipped.

"Whoa lil' mama, my bad for stating the obvious and telling you something you didn't know. He's had social media for a minute, though," I defended as I threw my hands up in the air.

"You are something else, Snow. On the real though, you reminded me of rapper Juvenile when you said that," she laughed.

"C'mere," I commanded in a low tone.

"I'm right here Snow, what you want me to do? Sit on your lap?" she looked me up and down.

Her eyes roamed over my face, then my chest, and onto my manhood. This woman was trying me for real. This would be the third time tonight that I caught her looking at my shit. Licking her full lips, she scooted in my direction. Her knee touched mine, so I grabbed her thigh and gently massaged it.

"Don't start nothing, Snow. I love just as hard as you do and this ain't what you want," she said seductively.

I moved my leg and pulled her closer to me, encasing her in a warm embrace. I knew that tonight wasn't the night for us to start anything with one another, solely because of the details of the situation surrounding her being here. Whispering in her ear, I told her something that every man should say to a woman before they consummate their relationship.

"I want to know you more. Most of all I want you to be ready for me emotionally, mentally, and physically because this monster gone have your head gone, bae," I smiled against her face and kissed her cheek sensually.

Chapter Thirteen
"In The Arms Of A Stranger"
Spencer

S taring at myself in the mirror, I didn't seem to recognize my own face. It had been a few months since I'd left Dominique for her ex-best friend Latrice.

Saying that I didn't miss her, would be a blatant lie. That girl cooked, cleaned, and fucked me whenever I wanted her to. Granted it wasn't the best I'd had, but I had been her first and her only. Fucking Latrice was a gamble, first the gonorrhea, now whatever the fuck this shit is.

A nigga had been feeling achy, nauseated, and had diarrhea for a while. Now my damn throat burns like hell, and looking at my tongue, I got this white shit piling up on it like a blanket of snow. It looked like that shit babies be having in their mouths. Thrush is the name of it, I think. Man, if this hoe gave me some shit, I'mma kill her in her muthafuckin' sleep. Being that we was together now, I wasn't playing that shit. However, it wouldn't be like she hadn't given me a disease before.

I decided to hop in the shower to wash off the night of sex we'd had. That hoe's pussy had been smelling a lil' rink. Nique's pussy always smelled and tasted like strawberries. It was like Tricey had given up on herself even more since she quit dancing due to her pregnancy. Nonetheless, I was happier than a baby in a barrel full of titties, simply knowing someone was carrying my seed. Even if it was a bitch without goals, dreams, or aspirations, my little one would carry on my legacy.

Being the man that I am, I wouldn't have wanted my baby's muva working anyway, especially not at a damn strip joint. The one thing I did despise was that she didn't wash her ass, cook, nor keep a clean house. I was constantly asking her to clean up the crib where all she did was watch *Love & Hip Hop*, *Housewives*, and *Black Ink Crew*, day in and day out.

"I gotta shit, won't you hurry up and get out the damn shower. You be in there longer than a bitch, I don't even shower that damn long." She was right, the only time she was in the shower was with me when I asked her to get in.

"You don't be in the shower at all. Go shit in the other bathroom with ya stank ass," I yelled through the door. I was getting fed up, she was becoming a thorn in my ass. She should've been close to four months along and still hadn't started to show yet.

I knew that pregnant women didn't need sanitary napkins or tampons, but when we packed her shit up to move in with me, there was no sign of them at her house. What did she use before she got pregnant?

Finally getting out of the shower, I smelled bacon and eggs cooking on the stove. Smiling to myself, I thought I had finally gotten through to her about cooking and cleaning. I had been in the bathroom long enough for her to have showered, cleaned the kitchen, and made breakfast. The kitchen was a disaster last night, it was like she'd used every dish in that muthafucka just to make macaroni and fried chicken. I didn't eat because the chicken was still bloody, and it ruined my appetite.

After sliding into my Under Armour basketball shorts, a white tee, and matching slides, I walked into the dining area and seated myself at the round dinner table. My stomach growled angrily, it was like the famine of a bear that was coming out of hibernation.

"Damn bae, that smells good as a bitch. I hope you hooked up enough for me too," I queried.

"There's a little leftover in there. You're welcome to put that shit on a plate and eat it," Tricey ranted and rolled her eyes.

Deciding to contain my anger, I got up and headed to the kitchen to fix my breakfast and was in for the shock of a lifetime. Dirty dishes were on the countertop, piled in the sink, and there was a pile of skillets and pots on the stove. She had awakened a beast in me. I had contained him for long enough.

Stalking over to her, I slapped the plate from her hand. Eggs went into one direction while the bacon and toast went another.

"Get the fuck up, Tricey. You got the same damn clothes on that you had on for the last two days, first off. Second, you went your nasty ass in there and cooked in the kitchen without cleaning that muthafucka. Today is your last muthafuckin' day of being trifling in this bitch."

She looked on in shock.

"What is your problem, nigga? I ain't Dominique's weak ass," she retorted with a scowl on her face.

"Muthafuckin' right you ain't. She would never walk around this bitch in the same damn clothes for days, not taking showers, nor cooking in a filthy ass kitchen. You could never be her, yo!" I yelled.

The hurt in her eyes should've made me feel bad. Instead, it made me want to punch her head in and not walk, but run back to Dominique. I knew that I had fucked things all the way up with her, but it didn't stop my heart from calling out to her.

Bzzz. Bzzz.

My celly vibrated against the glass table, breaking the staring match that Latrice and I were having. I wanted to drag her fuck ass into the kitchen and drown her in dish water. Instead, I decided to see who was in my inbox.

Lil Baby: I miss you daddy! (heart emoji)
Received 9:45 a.m.

I wanted to respond to her, but at the moment I was too upset with her fuck ass sister. I made a mental note to text her back whenever I freed myself from the arms of the stranger.

"Let me find out you still fuckin' that bitch and watch what happens to you... and her," she threatened.

"Yo, get the fuck on with your empty ass threats, for real shawty," I laughed in her face. "You know damn well you ain't 'bout that life. If Nique get off in your ass, you wouldn't know where to start to get up outta that lil' situation," I said between chuckles.

"Oh, you just on a roll comparing me to that bitch, huh? How you feel knowing that you lost her to your ex-best homie? You gotta feel like a nothing ass nigga losing your bitch to a white dude!" she shot back. It was now her time to laugh.

Snatching her up by her hair, I drug her ass to the kitchen, slamming her back against the wall. She looked at me with fear in her eyes, which only fueled my attack. I grabbed her by the throat and pinned her in place as she grabbed at my arms, scratching me and kicking her legs wildly. I'm sure my silence scared her more than anything as I stared her in the eyes.

"Let me go," she said through tears.

"Bitch, stop kicking because if you kick me, I'mma fuck you up in this bitch," I threatened.

"Let me the fuck go, Spencer," she begged.

"Bitch, you ain't got nowhere to go. Keep fuckin' with a real nigga and you gone be out on your nasty ass. Get this filthy ass kitchen cleaned up, take a shower, then take a damn bath. I can't believe you, you trifling hoe," I decided to let her down.

Walking off to get dressed, I was mentally ready to hit the streets on this beautiful Saturday morning. The bitch hit me in my back with a frying pan, breaking me from my thoughts. Why did she have to fuckin' do that? I turned to her with a deranged lunatic persona.

Grabbing her by the long ass weave she sported, I dragged her to the den. Once we got in there, I walked over to the radio taking my time to blast Kevin Gates's hit song, *In the Arms of a Stranger*.

The louder she screamed the more pissed I had become. I was sick of her shit and she had five more months before I could snatch my child from her for being an unfit mother. Until then, I would beat her ass senseless without harming my unborn.

Whap! Whap! Whap!

"Is this what you want?" I slapped her ass several times in the head and face.

"Stop hitting me!" she whimpered, causing me to hit her ass again.

"Nah, ain't no stop fuckin' hittin' you. You hit me in the back with a fuckin' frying pan, bitch. Next time finish the job," I yelled as I slapped her again.

"Please, I'm bleeding!" she cried.

Looking down at her, her face was a bloody mess. Her nose and lip were busted, and she had a bruise near her eye. I knew for sure she would be swollen in the morning, if not later today.

"Get this muthafuckin' house clean before I get back, and get ya nasty ass in the tub," I gritted. I shook my head in disgust and walked towards the master bedroom, more alert this time because I didn't want the bitch to pull another sneak attack on my ass.

$$$$

After riding around for a while, I decided to stop at *Mooyah's* Burger joint on Siegen Lane to get me some clean food. I had a feeling that I didn't get through to Latrice, so I didn't wanna risk going home without nourishment. That fuckin' Double Diablo burger was the shit. Walking into the restaurant, I already knew what I wanted so I stood patiently in line. The line typically moved fast so the fact that it was backed up to the door didn't deter me from changing up where I'd eat.

"Turkey Burger Club and a Loaded House Salad with extra bacon, for Wyatt," I heard the food prep lady call over the intercom. I started to ignore it, but then I remembered that each time Dominique and I would come here, she'd order that salad, the exact same way. I moved a little to my left and noticed Wyatt standing up from his booth toward the back of the restaurant.

"Ain't this about a bitch and his muva?" I grumbled.

"Right? This line is moving slow as hell today," the shorty in front of me turned to me tuning into my business.

"Yeah," I responded to not seem rude. She did have a nice lil' apple bottom on her.

Walking back to the booth, Wyatt sat the food down and slid into his seat. Just then he reached for the female he was out with and locked hands. They obviously prayed over their food, like some damn fools. I mean, who believed in a higher being. I don't know that nigga personally, never seen his ass, and I don't believe whoever wrote the mythical shit in the Bible knew him either.

That was one of Dominique's problems with me. She was no Christian by far, but she was a true believer that Jesus walked this earth and bestowed blessings upon us. I wasn't about to thank whoever he was for food I had to pay for, nor money and materialistic things I had to work for.

The revelation that Wyatt and Dominique were together now had bothered me. Fortunately, I had another chance at her heart because it was a lie. The girl that sat with him praying or chanting, or whatever they were doing, had honey-blonde natural hair. Nique always wore a sew-in. Plus, she would never damage her beautiful hair by processing it.

"Strawberry shake for Dommie," the same voice called over the intercom.

I looked around and didn't notice anyone moving, which caused me to look back to the corner. Just then the line started moving, bringing me closer to the register as well as their table. Lil' baby across from Wyatt hit his hand and he in turn, grabbed hers and kissed it. After a word exchange, she got up and walked to the counter.

My heart stopped beating at the sight of her. It was definitely Dominique and she was beautiful. She was smiling so brightly, and her happiness was almost contagious. The last few years of our relationship, I hadn't seen that. I had to admit it looked good on her. Her hair brought out the natural beauty she'd possessed. My heart raced at the thought of being back in her good graces again.

Making it to the front of the line, I ordered and paid for my meal. After the girl handed me my cup, I contemplated on whether or not I'd make my presence known. Within seconds, I was at the drink machine filling my cup up and rapping the lyrics to J. Cole's Nothing Lasts Forever.

Little sister hugs me
Even got a few homegirls that wanna fuck me
Soon as this shit ends forget about it
You been staying in my crib, you gotta get up out it

Being the petty nigga I am, I made sure to sing the part about the homegirls wanting to fuck me as loud as possible. After showcasing my lyrical talent in the form of covering a song, I noticed the looks on both their faces as they tried to divert their attention back to one another.

"What's up Nique? How you been doing, love, it's been a minute?" I asked, obliterating Wyatt's presence altogether.

Reaching for her hand, she snatched it away like I was the plague coming to infect her. Was she really gonna be like that with me? Her first and only true love...

"Ouch. That was a shot through the heart, love. That's how you gonna do me? I guess you don't love me no more for real, huh?" I probed.

"Nope. Truth is, I haven't loved you in a long time. For years, I was in love with the idea of you. You're just a woman-beating, womanizing thief that can't keep your diseased-dick in your pants," she looked at me in disgust.

"Ha. Ha. Ha. What's with you bitches today? First Latrice belittled me, now you!" I said and snatched her by the hair getting into her face.

I had completely zoned out, forgetting the fact that I was in a public place and that she was with Wyatt, a known scrapper. That was until he punched me in the jaw, causing me to release the grip I'd had on her. We were tearing that little corner up. I can't lie, he had the ups on me until I took the hot sauce bottle and busted him across the head with it.

He was still working me, but it was hard for him to keep up now that he was partially blinded by the liquid running into his eye. Just as I was about to go in for the kill, Dominique came from the south with a strong punch to the chest that winded me. Glad the bitch didn't get me in the face with her manly ass hit.

Wyatt regained his composure and we tussled for a few more moments before the police came in, breaking up the fight, and carting us off to the precinct.

$$$$

"Man, just drop me off at Mooyah's to get my damn car, yo!" I growled at Latrice. She was working a nigga's nerves, for real, for real.

"I will, why do you think I'm going towards Siegen, bae? I'm just tryna figure out why you and Wyatt was fighting, is all," she shot back. I guess she didn't understand that I was the one who asked questions.

Although she skated through the makeshift interrogation without an attitude, I didn't want her ass questioning me period. I popped in her Lil' Boosie cd and turned the volume up, I was done talking. Before long, we were pulling in next to my whip.

"Are you gonna come home tonight?" she asked.

"Yeah, I'll be there when I get there," I responded.

She leaned in with her lips puckered and I gave her a peck. She was my bitch, she could be sweet when she wanted to.

Hopping out of her car, I headed toward Jefferson Highway. I needed to see Nique, I had to explain and apologize to her for what I had done. I wanted to get back in good with her. When I was in holding, I thought about a lot of things. One being that I didn't know how to love a woman because my father never loved nor respected my mother. The crazy part is they weren't even together, and he still popped her every chance he'd gotten.

When I drove through the gate, I recognized Wyatt's truck going toward the exit. *How long has he been out?* I wondered. I didn't notice if Nique was in the car or not, but I kept my direction to her apartment.

Parking my ride, I got out and headed to the door. I knocked and rang the doorbell several times, yet I went unanswered. Remembering that I still had my key, I put it in the keyhole in an attempt to enter, but it was to no avail. She'd changed the locks. I gave up and headed home.

I decided to call Lestlee over my Bluetooth to talk to her during the ride to Sherwood.

"Hey daddy," she answered causing me to smile.

"Hey Lil' Baby. Daddy missed you," I responded.

"What's been up? I haven't heard from you in a minute. I know I've been busy with midterms, but why haven't you been calling or texting me?" Lestlee cooed into the phone.

"I can't lie, I been sick as fuck since I made it back from spending time with you two weeks ago. I think I got food poisoning or some shit."

"Me too. I've had diarrhea, nausea, chills and the most worrisome part is this thrush on my tongue. I thought only babies got that," she informed me of the same symptoms that I was having.

Although I knew I'd slowed up on fucking various bitches, I thought whatever I had, had come from her or that evil bitch, Tricey. We talked for a while longer and I told her that I was gonna go to the health unit to see what was up. She told me she had an appointment that Wednesday, to see what was going on.

After I'd pulled into my driveway next to my truck, I sat a few more minutes. She assured me that I was her only partner and I believed her. She was definitely in puppy love, this I knew for sure. She told me she loved me, I responded ditto and headed inside.

"Damn, it smells good in here. You did a good job, bae. I'm proud of you," I hugged my bruised and battered girlfriend, Latrice. She'd even cooked a full course meal which I was afraid to touch. I thought the bitch was trying to poison me for fucking her up earlier today.

"I'm sorry that I been a bitch to you, but this pregnancy is weighing on me. I don't have anyone but you, so you get all of me; the good, the bad, and the ugly," she kissed my lips sensually and led me to the bedroom.

Tricey pulled off my shirt and massaged my broad shoulders. I discreetly watched her ass through the mirror because I thought she was gonna try some slick shit. She started kissing my neck then got out of the bed and onto her knees. She gave me the best head of my muthafuckin' life.

"Get comfy, baby. I'mma take another shower then ride you like a cowgirl, so you can feed our seed," she winked and bit her thick bottom lip.

Doing as I was told, I stripped to my boxers and waited for her. No sooner than the water started, her phone vibrated several times, causing it to fall from the nightstand. I decided to do her a solid by getting outta the bed and picking it up.

The moment I'd had it in my hand, three messages came in back to back. Curiosity got the best of me, causing me to open her phone to take a peek. Scrolling to the beginning of the thread, it looked like some of the conversation had been erased. Being that she was team Android, I couldn't go in her deleted messages to find what was missing from the conversation.

Me: Bitch you better not tell a muthafuckin soul!
Message sent 8:56 p.m.
Cupcake: Bitch you crazy af for real
Message received 8:57 p.m.

I stopped to think of who the fuck Cupcake was. I thought a second longer and it donned on me that it was that fruity ass nigga that does the drag shows, that she's been hosting in downtown Baton Rouge on Freaky Friday's. Back to the message thread I went.

Me: I gotta go get this nigga outta jail bitch
Message sent 9:03 p.m.

Cupcake: u betta finish telling me about how he don't know u ain't preggers
Message received 9:31

Cupcake: Un un whore, u can't just tell a bitch how u gave him HIV to give to Dom's saditty ass and not finish telling me if the mission was accomplished
Message received 10:24 p.m.

Me: no bitch, mission failed because he left her for me. No baby for me because I had a hysterectomy when I was 18 and no HIV for her because they had stopped fucking a while ago, even though I fucked him when they were together we was using condoms at the time **crying emojis**
Message sent 10:26 p.m.

Me: He's home, I'll fwy toma luv I'm bout to suck this nigga dick and finish feeding him this HIV infested pussy. The grass ain't always greener for the pawns in a whore's game
Message sent 10:38 p.m.

Cupcake: well bitch, I guess the jokes on u hoe **crying laughing emojis**
Message received 11:01 p.m.

Cupcake: I can't believe u would do that to another queen no matter the circumstances smh
Message received 11:01 p.m.

Cupcake: **thinking emojis** biiiiiitch, FYI I don't like yo ass, never did honestly. But I couldn't put my finger on why. Now I know why I only tolerated u it's because u's a dirty ass bitch. Although I never liked Dom, that girl loved u like a sister. Yo dusty ass used to wear her clothes until she started buying yall matching shit. SMMFH. U know, taking her man was 1 thing but this... u took hatred to a whole nother level. I'mma screenshot this and share it on all of my SM Accts... look for the tags and the fallout... slutty diseased dying whore.
Message received 11:02 p.m.

I sat there blowing my top. I knew I couldn't be reading what the fuck I thought I was reading. This couldn't be life for the kid, I know that this was a sick joke she was playing because she knew I would check her phone. I'm 'bout to kill this bitch. No sooner than that thought crossed my mind, she exited the bathroom in just a t-shirt.

"You ready to fuck this go–" she cut her question short when she realized I had her phone in my hand.

She took off running down the hallway, but I caught up to her ass. Her actions proved that everything I had read was true. Before I realized it, I had beat her ass so bad that she had to drive herself to the hospital with a broken arm.

Chapter Fourteen
"Pose'd To Be In Love"
Sharae Latrice

This bitch Cupcake fell through with his promises to out me. It had been two weeks since I'd been laid up in this hospital and I was ready to go home.

I lied and told the police that I had a fight at the club and was jumped by four unknown females. As bad as Spence had fucked me up, it was believable. I had six broken ribs, a broken eye socket, a broken arm, and two missing teeth. I wasn't too much worried about the teeth because I fucked with a dentist who would fix that. That was if he hadn't seen all of the shit on social media about me.

After everything had fallen through the cracks, I knew life for me would change drastically. All kinds of people were calling my room, sending death threats to my social media inbox, and stopping by. When the smoke cleared, and all of this shit started to set in, I only wanted three people at my side; My sister Lestlee, my ex-best friend Dominique, and the only nigga that ever gave a fuck about me, Spencer. Although I had taken Spencer under false pretenses, he did show me love. That was the reason I couldn't hate him for what he'd done to me. Really, for the way he'd responded to what I'd done to him.

Ring. Ring. Ring.

The phone at my bedside rang, jolting me from my thoughts. I was afraid to answer because I figured it would be another death threat or someone full of hatred.

"Hello?" I answered. It was more so a question of who the fuck was on my line than an inviting answer.

"Hey baby," I heard a voice I hadn't heard in almost two years.

"Oh, it's you. How'd you know I was here?" I responded slyly.

"Look, I know your upbringing play a major role in what's going on witchu right now. I didn't call to fight witchu, I called to see if I could step in and start anew. I need you just as much as you can use me. I mean regardless, I am yo' mama," she explained.

There was a brief silence. It was so quiet on the line that all we could do was hear one another breathing. For moments I cried in silence, the truth was I did need her. Sadly, I acknowledged that I needed her long before today.

"I needed you years ago, you know when I was your meal ticket, the pawn in your sick and twisted little scheme to get money by any means necessary. I needed you to love me, to teach me how to love and be loved. Up until I started sleeping with the man I intentionally infected, I only knew the love of money," I sobbed. "Mama, I needed you. I needed you to teach me how to be a woman," I was at a loss and didn't know where to take the conversation, so I simply cried.

"Tricey, I'm sorry. I'm sorry for everything that I have ever exposed you to in your life. On God, I'm sorry that I did those horrible things to you." That was new, I'd never heard her mention God. "This is no excuse, however, I need you to know that it was the lack of parenting on my parents' part that drove me to do those things. I won't fully blame them because I had a mind of my own and I should've known that what I was doing was wrong," she cried.

I didn't know if I should believe her or not. I hadn't seen or heard from her parents since the last time they had paid our rent, I was six years old at the time. Mama had been approved for low-income housing, freeing them from the responsibility of affording her housing, to keep a roof over our heads. The last words I'd heard my grandmother say stuck with me throughout my life.

"You're a low-life. You have these two beautiful girls to raise you gonna have to learn independence. Me and my husband will no longer help you financially. And you better not dare fix your mouth to ask me to babysit these snotty-nosed brats."

That shit stuck to me like hot grits to a cheating ass nigga. It was then that I knew that life was gonna be rough for us. Mama didn't work, she depended on them to pay her way for everything. Granny had told her that they would be cutting her off at twenty-one, yet they had given her another full year of support, because that visit was the day before her twenty-second birthday.

"Tricey?" she queried.

"Yup, I'm still here," I responded. I questioned her motive.

What did she truly want? Was it money, because I didn't have shit but the car that I'd recently paid off. That was all thanks to the lick we'd hit at Dominique's apartment. That was some fucked up shit on both our parts, however, we did it. I was in a bad way at the time.

"Do you feel up for some company? I'm sure you'll be there for a while," she asked.

"Sure," I responded after a moment. I decided to allow her here so that I could look in her eyes, merely to see if I noticed anything flaw about her or her intentions.

I had been texting Spence day in and day out following my surgeries. He was livid. At one point all he did was send me the middle finger emojis, which meant that he still cared. Now, he wouldn't respond at all, it had been about ten days. I was worried that I'd lost him indefinitely. Of course, there were support groups and even dating websites to go to in order to find love in people of my likes but, I only wanted him.

Yes, I had HIV and yes I had hurt him in a horrible way when all he did was fall in love with a broken bitch. I needed him like the world needed it's mix of good air and bad air to level itself out. He was oxygen and I was carbon dioxide.

Deciding to scroll on my Instagram page, the drama was still crazy, but it had died down a tad bit. Everybody and their mothers said that they'd be waiting on my release so that they could take me out before the AIDS did. At first I was like let me out now, but after talking with several counselors and life coaches, I wanted to live to see the better days.

Deciding to watch television, I had tuned into the *Maury Povich Show*. Coincidentally, the topic was *Is My Best Friend Sleeping With My Husband*. I had to laugh at the irony, however, I tuned in. By the end of the show, I was in tears. The depth of what I had not only done to Spencer, but what I had done to my own best friend had weighed on me and I felt like shit.

I finally realized that what I'd done was wrong and decided to shoot Nique a text asking her to come up to visit me so that I could talk to her and tell her what was up.

> **Me:** Hey Dom it's me. I know you don't fwm and all but I really need to clear the air
>
> *Message sent 5:03 p.m.*
>
> **Rich Saditty Bitch:** I could be petty and tell you all the reasons why Idgaf but I won't. What's your room number?
>
> *Message received 5:07 p.m.*
>
> **Me:** 403, I'm on the A side where they keep the oncology people. Thank you for coming.
>
> *Message sent 5:07 p.m.*

I was excited that she agreed to come to see me. I felt a relief to be able to tell her in my own words what I had done and why I'd done it. I knew she had seen and read all of the posts that were floating around. Some asshole had even made memes with my pictures on them. One of the captions read, "Even if it means getting the best head of your life before you die, just do it". I was like, what the fuck does that even mean?

I had taken a nap to pass time being that I didn't know what time either my mom or Dom was going to make it up here. No sooner than I started to dream of the best sex I'd ever had, I felt someone tapping my foot. Before opening my eyes, I knew it was Clara Louise, my mother. I'd smelled her perfume, I couldn't believe she still wore that hideous smelling crap.

"Hey baby girl, I know you ain't sleep cuz I see yo' eyes moving," she laughed. Her voice so soft, yet raspy. It was just as I'd remembered. I had no choice but to smile, I couldn't hide my excitement any longer.

"Hey mama," I greeted. I discreetly eyed her full body as she had gained a bit of weight. She went from being Cardi B thick, to Niecey Nash thick... it looked good on her.

Walking over to hug me, I warned her against it telling her what was going on with me. She said that I was her child and she didn't care. She said if I had SARS she was gonna hug and kiss me. That made me feel worthy.

"It's been a long time, baby. I know I said this over the phone, but I wanted to tell you in person, so that you can see my eyes." *Damn she must've read my mind,* I thought. "I want to start by saying I sincerely apologize to you for everything that I allowed you to endure. I won't speak about Lestlee because that's a hatchet that I'd have to bury with her," she breathed. "What I did and allowed others to do to you was wrong and I'm sorry for everything."

When the tears fell, and she tightened the grip on my hand, I knew she was sincere and it was then that I had decided to forgive her.

"I love you baby, I always have. I admit that I wasn't the best, hell, I wasn't even good. I want you to know that now that I know better, I'mma do better," she kissed my fingers.

After we talked for a bit, I found out that she'd been to rehab, had gotten a certified in crime scene investigation, and had just gotten accepted into Southern University's school of Nursing. She was going to school to become a forensic nurse, I thought that was pretty dope. To say I was proud of her would be an understatement. I was surprised to see the growth and maturity in my mother. I was half her age and it took all of my life for her to get it together, but she did.

"Mama, thank you for coming up here today," I couldn't allow her to leave without saying thank you. I was an ungrateful bitch to a lot of people and it was time I'd changed the input, so I could change the output. Maybe if I'd altered how I viewed the world, the world would change how it viewed me.

"No need to thank me baby, I will be up here every day until you either get tired of seeing me or they let you outta here." Kissing my forehead, she grabbed my hands once again and stared me in the eye before she'd let the tears flow freely. "I'm sorry I failed you, I promise I am."

Picking up her keys, she headed to the door just as someone knocked and entered before either of us had a chance to respond.

"Hey Mama Clara, you looking like a whole meal, lady. How have you been?" I heard Dominique's voice in the distance to the door.

"Hey baby, nice to see you. I like your hair, I see you finally wearing that beautiful mane out and have colored it, huh! Look at you go." They laughed.

"I guess that's what a dope love will do for you. It was nice seeing you here," Dominique responded.

"I see. Love sure looks good on you baby, take care."

My mother had always loved Dominique and she loved her. Regardless to the way she'd raised us, she had her moments of being good and that was what Dom saw, aside from what I cried to her about.

In that moment I felt like shit. I thought about every secret Dominique had ever kept and everything that she had ever done. That girl had bought for me, fought for me, and even talked for me. Whereas, the only thing I'd done was the worst of the worst to try to hurt her, all in return for her merely loving me.

"Hey Tricey." Dominque finally made it to my bedside. Sitting near me she eyed me intently and looked as if she felt empathetic. After all I'd done, she still had love in her heart for me.

"Hey Dominique," I responded as sadness filled my main organ. As I looked at her, the course of our friendship replayed a thousand and one times in my head. Not one scenario had revealed that she had ever wronged me. "I'm sorry sis," I cried.

I was in a mess of emotions. Even with HIV status, Nique grabbed my hand and held it tight as I cried all of my tears. I thought of a million ways to explain to her what I had done and why I had done it. But, I couldn't bring myself to tell her that I had intentions of harming her, in a way that I had attempted. Although I knew she had seen the posts that had flooded social media, I couldn't find my own words.

"I forgive you for everything that you did to me," she said as if she'd read my mind. "I need to go to the restroom, I'll be right back."

That was too simple, I needed to tell her. I desperately wanted to free myself of the hinderance of my heart, mind, and morale.

After moments had passed, the door opened to my room. "I thought you weren't coming back," I laughed.

"I shouldn't have, but I love you. Sadly, I too need to confess some shit," Spencer said as he took the same seat that Dominique and my mother had previously sat in.

"I love you too. I may have not realized the depth of my dirt until all of this happened and I'm sorry," I admitted. "Dominique just left, I thought you were her. She was supposed to be going to the restroom," I advised Spence of the possible confrontation.

"I got this for you," Dominique said as she rounded the corner with a large candy bouquet and balloons placing it on the table near the wall. She knew I'd die for the candy bouquet. Just like any real friend, she remembered my vices. "I know that your favorite is Kit-Kat, but they were running low on those, so I had them fill it with the remainder of them along with Snickers and Butterfinger. I also remember that you were a white lily type of chick, so I had to go across the str–"

Her rant was cut short by the sight of Spencer, who had dropped my hand. After standing to his feet to face her, she'd walked over to the bed looking from me to him and him to me. The look of hurt and betrayal was ever-present, and I felt the pang of it in my heart. I'd been the one responsible for this, I owed her my loyalty and I had cut her real deep with the hatred I'd built up because her life, was seemingly better than mine.

"No need to stand, I'm over everything that you've both done to me. All I had ever tried to do was be good to both of you. I knew you were cheating but I had never assumed you'd go so low as to sleep with someone I'd considered my own sister," she paused. "I knew the type of person you were but never had I imagined I'd be a victim of your uncanny promiscuous behavior. I loved you like the sister I'd never had," she hugged me and kissed my forehead.

"Dominique, please let me explain," I begged.

"Nah, there's no need. I'm good love, you bitches enjoy."

With those words, she turned to walk out on both me and Spencer. Turning back around to face me, she had a slight frown etched on her beautiful face. I can't lie, it scared the living shit out of me because everyone knows by now, a bitch can't fight.

"Dominique, I ma–" Spencer was cut off when she threw her manicured finger up and shook her head.

"I'mma need this right here though," she informed me and snatched her grandmother's cross from my neck. "You can keep this," she said dropping the broken necklace onto my lap after pulling the pendant from it.

I was broken. After everything, she was willing to forgive me. Yet when she came in to see Spencer holding my hand, I was sure that I'd lost her indefinitely.

Chapter Fifteen
Forgive Me For My Disrespect, Forgive Me For My Lies
Lestlee

"Are you trying to get me pregnant?" I asked after our third round of sex. Spencer had been in Miami with me for almost a month now. To say he didn't want any attachments, he surely had a way of making me think he cared about me more than he did Nique or my sister.

There were a few times that we hadn't used condoms since we started having sex, but he'd be sure to make me take my birth control, and we'd kept Morning After pills on deck. Now, we'd stopped using protection completely, we hadn't used any since the first week he made it here. I'd missed my appointment at the clinic because he'd made it here on Tuesday evening and had only let me out of sight for finals. Whatever ailment I'd had was gonna have to wait, he said.

"Fuckin' well right, you my bitch. I need everyone on campus to know that you off the market," Spence replied before kissing me in the mouth. I loved and hated that he referred to me as his bitch rather than his girlfriend, but I wouldn't fight him on it. Instead, I smiled and pushed up off of him to head to the shower.

He'd rented a condo on the beach for us so that Neekie, my nosey ass roommate, wouldn't hear us fucking like rabbits. They'd met each other finally, however they didn't mesh well. She'd said he was up to no good and wondered what he wanted with me, being that he was ten years my senior. She was simply hating because he bought me a Prius and kept my pockets filled with cash.

"Where you going Lee?" he grabbed my arm aggressively.

"Ouch, why you have to grip my arm like I'm running away or something? I'm headed to the shower. We been fucking all morning and neither of us has cleaned up," I responded.

"I'm sorry lil' baby. It's just that I been getting hurt by the women in my life lately and I'm on edge," he looked at me with distress in his eyes and I felt some type of way. However, that didn't deter me from my shower. I was clean, always have been and always will be.

I let that one slide because I knew that he'd been going through some shit. My sister said Nique put them hands on him not long ago, which I'd always wondered why she allowed him to beat her anyway. Grabbing my things, I headed to the shower.

After I'd showered and gotten dressed, I stood in the mirror and noticed that my body was drastically different. My mouth had ulcers in it, the body aches were crazy, and my cooch was leaking like no tomorrow. It was the worst yeast infection that I'd ever had in life, even *Monistat* wasn't working for it. My skin had been needing extra moisturizer because it was dry and flaky, which it had also been producing scaly-looking blisters.

I was happy to had gotten an appointment at the doctor's office to find out what had been going on with me. "Hey babe, I'm gonna head on over to the clinic," I informed Spencer.

"Clinic?" he questioned as if he'd forgotten about the appointment that I had to reschedule.

"Yeah, to see what this is that's attacking my body. I've been so damn tired lately and look at me... I've lost weight and these little sores are popping up like pop-up shops at the Essence Festival," I said, trying to make light of the situation.

Walking up to me, he'd lifted my shirt up and inspected my back, which I found odd. *How'd he know exactly where to search for the blisters?* I thought. I brushed it off and headed out before I was late and had to reschedule again.

"Ok love, I won't be here when you get back. I need to get back to B.R. Because I got shit to handle," he kissed me and started to pack his things. "I got this house for three months so if you wanna stay here, I'll be back and forth until the lease is up."

"Nah, I don't like to be alone. Whenever you come back, I will definitely make my way here, so I can be naked and waiting," I said seductively.

"Bet," was all he said.

$$$$

"Bitch, you look like shit!" My roommate turned friend informed me. For some reason or another, I couldn't beat the hacking cough that's been so disrespectful to me and my throat. Of all of the symptoms, the night sweats were the worst. I thought I'd had the flu, but I'd been swabbed for it when I went to the clinic last week and it came back negative.

It was now day ten since I'd had a full metabolic panel run on my blood. I was anxious because I hadn't received any news. "Girl fuck you, I look better than you," I laughed but she didn't. I had laughed so hard that the coughing attack had come back full-fledged. I had a metallic taste in my mouth but I hadn't produced any blood.

As I got up to get a drink of water to cure my dry throat and possibly ease my cough, I lost my bowels. It had to be the absolute most embarrassing moment of my life. I ran to the bathroom with a trail of shit following me. When I got to the restroom, I was able to pull my pants down and sit on the toilet. Unfortunately the shit-filled evening was just getting started.

After sitting on the toilet for what felt like forever, and killing the nerves in both my legs, I'd finally stopped shitting long enough to shower and go into the living room to clean up behind myself. Neekie was a good friend. Although she'd left the house, she had cleaned up the mess and left a note saying that my phone had been ringing off the hook.

Stalking over to my phone, I noticed that I'd had several missed calls and text messages from Spencer, Tricey, and an unknown caller. After reading all the texts from them, I decided to listen to the voicemails. The first one was from Tricey asking me to call her about something important. Next few was from Spencer asking me to call him because he needed to get something off of his chest. Then the last one that I'd listened to was from the clinic. My results were in, they'd called me to set an appointment to come in to discuss my results.

I was so nervous waiting for the day to pass that I'd literally fallen asleep with my phone charging in my hand. Hearing the door open, I jolted out of my sleep only to see my drunken roommate stumbling into the living room with some guy on her heels.

"Shhhh, we might wake up my shitty-ass friend. Oops, I didn't mean to say that. I love that bitch," a sad look consumed her as I peeked over my blanket.

"Why'd you call her that? Is she mean or some shit?" the guy asked with a Baton Rouge accent. She always fell in line for Louisiana dudes, which was beside me. Them niggas did two things: Listen to the local rapper Scottie Cain and drive around the city in their baby mama's cars.

"Never mind, I didn't mean to say that about her. We fuckin' or nah?" she slurred.

"Hell yeah we are, let's tag her in!" his greed for pussy exuded through his diamond grill.

"You know what, nigga? Get the fuck out! You won't disrespect me or her. How the fuck you think she would feel if I woke her up asking her for a threesome with me and a random ass nigga? Get the fuck out of our shit!" she screamed.

"Bitch, I'll bat the fuck outta you talking to me like you stupid," he raised his hand up to hit her and I jumped up from the chaise, grabbing the bat that we kept in our living room for intruders.

"You heard what the fuck she said. Now, get yo' fake Mista Cain looking ass the fuck up outta here fo' a bitch bash yo' brain in, nigga!" I gritted as I held the bat tightly, ready to Babe Ruth his ass.

After we'd gotten the situation under control, we sat down to catch our breaths. "Friend, I don't know if you heard what I said about you, but I really didn't mean it. They say drunkards speak sober minds, but I really didn't have cruel intentions following what I said," she teared up.

"It's all good. I'm worried about my health though. I don't know what to think of it, I hated looking at Google because that bitch will have you thinking that you are HIV positive with six days left to live," we laughed. "I still love you boo!"

"Love you more, that's on Foe Nem!" When I heard her use of Chicago slang which meant *on everything*, I knew she was being one hunnit with me.

$$$$

I left the clinic with tears in my eyes and hatred in my heart. Someone was gonna pay for what they'd done. After talking with Tricey over the phone this morning on the way to hear my results, she still hadn't told me what was going on, just that she had booked an open-ended flight for me to make it to the Louis Armstrong airport whenever I could.

Deciding to take her up on her offer, I hopped on the next flight out. I'd made it from New Orleans to Baton Rouge in record time. Coincidentally, my seat partner was headed there to visit her sick grandfather at Baton Rouge General. I remembered Tricey saying she'd moved so I texted her from the hospital asking for the new address. Shortly following, I hailed a cab and showed up to her new crib in Sherwood.

Ding. Dong.

I rang the doorbell and waited. Within moments, my sister opened the door with a smile on her face, pulling me into a hug. "What happened to your grill, sis? Somebody finally kicked your ass for fucking their man, huh?" I laughed at her missing teeth, but she didn't.

"No, stupid ass girl," she had to be mad because she never in life called me stupid. It was a word that she dared me to use in her presence.

"Well, that escalated quickly. What's wrong with you?" I asked as we broke from our hug.

"Look, I asked you to come here because I have very important news to share with you. Come in and get comfy because it's gonna take some time," she insisted.

Walking into her home, it was pristine. I definitely wasn't used to her house being this clean because Tricey was a slob. All she knew how to do was fuck a nigga and get some money, I was the maid. I didn't complain because I didn't have to do anything but cook and clean for her to keep me fresh to death and my pockets loaded with cash.

After dropping the bomb on me about what was going on with her and what she tried to do to Nique, I was at a loss for words. I lost my breath knowing that I was a pawn in Spence's game as he was a pawn in hers.

"Babe, I got us food from Village Grocery, I know how much you li-" Spence's statement was cut by the sight of me sitting in the den area with my sister, Tricey. "H-h-h-hey Lestlee. W-w-w-what you doing in our neck of the woods?" he stuttered.

At that moment, I was so glad that I had stopped at my homie Big E's house, to get me a hot gun. I trekked to the living room to my bag to fetch my results and my new pistol.

"Lee, where are you going?" Tricey called out. I ignored her with tears staining my foundation and my t-shirt. "What the hell is wrong with her?" Tricey asked Spencer. He knew but he damn sure wasn't gonna say.

After stalking my way back to the den, they both sat at a card table looking at each other in suspense. I slammed my results on the wooden slate, eyeing them both intently. "You dirty muthafuckas is the reason for this shit. Here I came to warn you of his bullshit, and it was you all along." Tears flowed so heavily that they clouded my vision.

"You don't wanna do this!" Spencer yelled.

Tricey was at a loss for words, she looked as if she didn't understand.

"But I do, you dirty dick bitch!" I violently wiped the tears that filled my eyes. "Tell me why, huh? Why the fuck would you do that to me when you knew all along," I called out.

"What am I missing?" Tricey looked between us.

Cocking the hammer back on a gun I had had a five-minute training on, I pointed it back and forth between the two of them.

"Please Lee, let me explain to both of y'all yo. Don't kill a nigga!" Spencer begged.

"Nah, fuck ass nigga. Because of y'all nasty asses, we are all walking dead. This right here," I brandished the weapon recklessly. "Will help me to speed up the process, y'all don't deserve to see better days."

Pow! Pow! Pow! Pow!

To be continued...

It has definitely been a journey. Book number four and I really am still in shock mode. I can't believe this dream of mine is now a reality. The Magnificent Seven and I appreciate you all for riding this thing out with us. Hope you all stay on until the wheels fall off... I will keep dropping stories until my alter ego won't produce anymore. Thank you to my family and friends. God bless you all, much love.

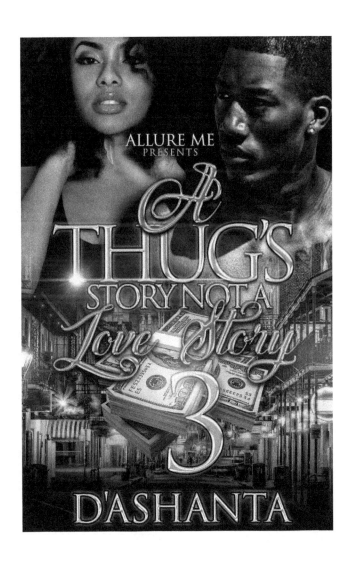

ALLURE ME
PRESENTS

A THUG'S STORY NOT A Love Story 3

D'ASHANTA

Coming
09/24/2018

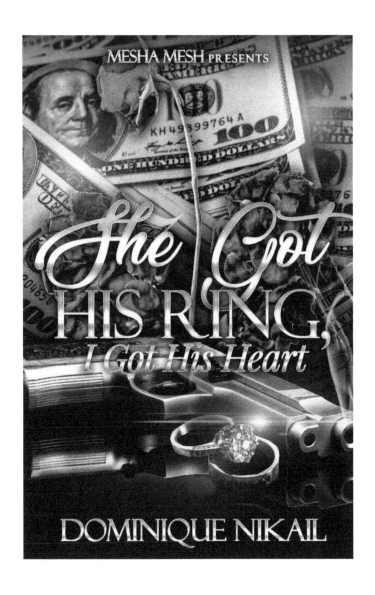

Coming
10/01/2018